Duke Sothbridge's Vessel

S. Rodman

Dark Angst Publishing

Copyright © 2023 by S. Rodman

All rights reserved.

No portion of this book may be reproduced in any form without written permission from the publisher or author, except as permitted by U.S. copyright law.

ISBN: 9798386680565

Cover design by Miblart.

ALL RIGHTS RESERVED: This literary work may not be reproduced or transmitted in any form or by any means, including electronic or photographic reproduction, in whole or in part, without express written permission.

All characters and events in this book are fictitious. Any resemblance to actual persons living or dead is strictly coincidental.

WARNING: The unauthorized reproduction or distribution of this copyrighted work is illegal. Criminal copyright infringement, including infringement without monetary gain, is investigated by the FBI and is punishable by up to 5 years in federal prison and a fine of $250,000.

This book contains,

Dubious consent

Reference to past child sexual abuse

Near sharing with dubious consent

Accidental facial injury which is assumed to be domestic violence

Forced confinement

A scene where murder is plotted

Reference to past sexual assault inflicted by a main character on a side character

Contents

1. Chapter 1   1
2. Chapter 2   7
3. Chapter 3   13
4. Chapter 4   19
5. Chapter 5   23
6. Chapter 6   29
7. Chapter 7   39
8. Chapter 8   45
9. Chapter 9   49
10. Chapter 10   55
11. Chapter 11   61
12. Chapter 12   67
13. Chapter 13   71
14. Chapter 14   79
15. Chapter 15   83

16.	Chapter 16	87
17.	Chapter 17	93
18.	Chapter 18	99
19.	Chapter 19	103
20.	Chapter 20	111
21.	Chapter 21	117
22.	Chapter 22	121
23.	Chapter 23	127
24.	Chapter 24	133
25.	Chapter 25	141
26.	Chapter 26	147
27.	Chapter 27	153
28.	Chapter 28	161
29.	Chapter 29	167
30.	Chapter 30	175
	Thank You	181
	The Prince's Vessel	183
	Books By S. Rodman	185

Chapter One

This is it. My last chance to have a decent life. If I blow this moment. I blow everything.

The ballroom goes all blurry. Sound goes all fuzzy. The only thing I can hear clearly is my heartbeat pounding in my ears. I hope my palms aren't sweaty, because that would be gross.

My phone slides out of my trembling fingers. It drops onto the smooth wooden floor with a thud loud enough to wake the dead. How has no one heard it? It seems miracles do happen. I just need to keep walking. Okay, here is a good spot. Stop, turn around. Smile. Pretend to be watching the dancers on the floor and breathe.

Duke Rakeswell is still making his way towards the refreshments. A few more steps and he is going to pass my phone. Lady Buxley just needs to stop talking to him and everything will be fine.

"Colby?"

I jump out of my skin.

Duke Sothbridge is standing right in front of me. I blink but he is still here. I'm not seeing things. He looks jaw droppingly stunning as ever. Tall, tanned, blond, muscled. Striking aquamarine eyes that seem to dazzle with his every naughty thought.

Such a shame he is an evil creep.

"Your Grace," I reply politely.

"You are growing up to be a good-looking young man," he comments, as his eyes rake over my entire body as if they are undressing me.

I shudder. The audacity of the man to sound surprised. How dare he! And he saw me three months ago at Earl Somerset's garden party. How one grows in three months is beyond me. His comment implies that he has never noticed me before or that he is simply saying it for an excuse to be a letch. Both reasons are intolerable.

Out of the corner of my eye, I can see Duke Rakeswell approaching my phone. I need to get rid of Sothbridge and I need to do it now.

"Thank you, your grace. It's so wonderful to see you looking so well after your duel with Lord Garrington."

It's ancient history. Long forgotten. There have been countless scandals in society since and nobody cares anymore. But it has the desired effect. Sothbridge scowls at me and walks away.

What a relief.

Rakeswell sees my phone and picks it up. My heart is pounding again. He touches the screen. I spent hours and hours choosing the selfie for the lock screen. I hope he likes it and agrees that I look absolutely charming in it. I know any selfie would have done, he just needs to know the phone is mine. But, you know, no harm in reminding him how cute I am.

His gaze starts to sweep the ballroom. Looking for me. Time for me to drift closer to Lady Connham and her sisters whilst pretending I'm engrossed by the dancers on the floor.

I risk a sideways peek and nearly shriek in delight. Rakeswell is striding towards me. I have to time this perfectly. Okay, now, he is close enough and clearly approaching me.

"Oh! Your grace! I'd love to dance!" I gush at the top of my voice, as I place my hands over my heart for good measure.

I've certainly gained Connham and her sisters' attention.

Rakeswell looks completely taken aback for a moment, but he nods sharply, slips my phone into his pocket and offers me his arm instead. Perfect.

He is too nice to embarrass me by calling me out on my misunderstanding. I knew it. Tonight's plan is going to work flawlessly. A shiver of guilt traces up my spine as he sweeps me onto the dancefloor. But it's not an evil plan. I'm pretty sure Rakeswell likes me, and he does need a vessel. And I need to be married before everyone finds out about my family's financial situation. So it's a win-win for both parties. Rakeswell just needs a little incentive, a little pushing in the right direction. I'm sure he would have proposed eventually, if my family fortune hadn't taken a tumble, so all I'm really doing is hurrying things along. There is no need to feel bad.

Dancing with Rakeswell is nice. The feel of his hand on the small of my back is bliss. He is a good-looking man, and he is inches away. Part of myself is screaming at me to climb him like a tree but I take a deep breath instead. I've been perpetually horny for years. Horny and unsatisfied. I can handle it.

As I execute a perfect turn, I catch my mother's gaze. She nods at me. She is ready.

I stumble clumsily into Rakeswell and his grip on me tightens.

"Are you alright?" he asks with a small frown.

Time to look up at him and flutter my eyelashes, "I... I feel a bit faint."

His frown deepens, and his brown eyes fill with concern. But he is just staring at me as we stand motionless on the dancefloor.

"Fresh air?" I prompt.

"Oh gosh! Yes, of course!"

Finally he is taking me outside to the gardens. The cool night air is refreshing. It's surprisingly mild for October. There are a few other people dotted around, talking in small groups and enjoying either the fresh air or a cigarette. Perfect. I need witnesses.

I bend over and groan dramatically. "Oh, I'm going to be sick!"

Rakeswell grip on my arm tightens even more.

"Please take me over there!" I gasp. Waving a hand weakly at the entrance of the hedge maze. "I don't want anyone to see me being sick!"

I stare at him imploringly, in desperation. I'm sweating with nerves, hopefully it's just convincing him that I really am sick.

He springs into motion, half dragging, half carrying me to the maze. As we step inside, I whimper and make a gross retching noise. He stops. I bend over some more. We are a little further into the maze than I would have liked, but I think mother and her friends will still be able to see us when they stroll past in a moment.

"What's wrong with him?"

The voice makes me whip my head round. Sothbridge is strolling out of the depths of the maze. His shirt and tie are all undone and he has a vape hanging from the corner of his mouth. With his hands shoved in his pockets, he looks the very picture of nonchalant arrogance.

"He is sick!" exclaims Rakeswell, sounding near hysterical with concern.

What a sweetheart. I've chosen well. He is going to be an excellent husband.

"Help him, while I fetch him some water!"

Wait! What? No! I stare in horror at the sight of Rakeswell running at full speed out the maze. Damn that man is fast. I didn't have a chance to say a word.

My gaze flicks to Sothbridge. He frowns and gives me a very suspicious look. My heart is not beating, it's thrumming. I open my mouth to say something.

"Oh my goodness!" shrieks mother at the top of her lungs.

She has managed to bring a whole frigging retinue over. The ladies all start squealing and shrieking in shock at the sight of me alone in the maze with Duke... Sothbridge. It was meant to be Rakeswell. It was supposed to be Rakeswell.

My horrified gaze snaps back to Sothbridge. His disheveled state would have been perfect if he was the right duke. He has clearly been having fun with someone.

Sothbridge's face fills with icy fury.

"You little bastard!" he snarls.

I swallow. I think I might actually be sick now. In front of everyone. I can't bear to look, but it sounds like everyone in the world has rushed over to see what all the commotion is about.

Oh no! I'm still bending over! Hastily I straighten up but it's far, far too late.

My life is over.

Chapter Two

Father is sitting in his chair dabbing at his eyes with a red spotted handkerchief. Mother is standing behind him, one hand squeezing his shoulder reassuringly.

Father's study should be a familiar, comforting space, but the world has changed. Nothing is the same. Nothing will ever be the same again.

I was discovered alone, in a dark maze with Duke Sothbridge. It was hours ago now, it must be. It is a three-hour journey between Humberland House, where the ball was, and home. But I think I'm still in shock because it feels like no time has passed at all. I can't remember a thing about the drive back.

"What are we going to do," sobs Father.

"Shh," says Mother. "It's going to be fine, Sothbridge will propose. He has to."

"He won't!"

"Of course he will, all that nasty business with Lord Garrington's Vessel on the balcony? His reputation has already taken a hit, he cannot weather another one."

My throat is tight. I can't swallow. I don't want Duke Sothbridge to propose. He is horrid. He assaulted a vessel on a balcony and had the audacity to declare that gave him the right to claim him. Sothbridge is nothing like sweet Rakeswell. Sothbridge is arrogant. Sothbridge is cruel. Sothbridge has a different man in his bed every night. He would make a terrible husband.

"Rakeswell is giving his word that Colby was sick and he only left him alone with Sothbridge to fetch some water."

Mother frowns, "I know he was only trying to help, but saying Colby was alone with two mages doesn't make the situation any better."

"Maybe Rakeswell will propose?" I interject hopefully.

"You were seen with Sothbridge and he is the one with the reputation," says my mother, dashing all my hopes and dreams.

"Sothbridge won't propose! He is a fiend! Our boy is ruined! We are ruined!" wails Father.

Oh gosh. Maybe I do want Sothbridge to propose. Father is right. It's Sothbridge or no one. I was on the shelf before this, add in a scandal and no one will ever want me. And that's before everyone discovers we are now poor.

I'm going to be alone forever. I'm going to die a virgin. A poor virgin. It's a tragedy.

A knock on the door makes me jump out of my skin. Jeeves walks in with a very fancy letter on a silver tray. He presents it to my father. The study falls silent. I don't think anyone is breathing.

With trembling fingers, Father picks up the thick, gilded paper and unfolds it. I watch his eyes scan the contents and then he looks at me but I can't decipher his expression.

"Sothbridge has proposed."

I can't see. I can't hear. Reality has fallen away. I'm stunned and I don't know what to think. I should be happy, shouldn't I? I should be ecstatic. This is wonderful news. It solves all our problems. It is the best possible outcome.

I've been trying my best to get someone to propose to me for years now. Ever since my nineteenth birthday and the official mourning period had passed. A proposal has been my only goal in life for three long years. So why am I swamped by this feeling? This feeling that feels suspiciously like terror.

An image flashes of Sothbridge's face when we were discovered.

'You little bastard!' he had snarled.

I think I'm going to faint. He is furious at me. He hates me. He is going to be my husband and my master. I'm a vessel, he is a mage. That means he is going to take my body to take my magic.

It's going to be nothing like an arranged marriage between mundanes. We won't be able to ignore each other. He will want my magic, so I will have to surrender my body to him whenever I'm ripe.

I shiver. I pray to any and all gods that I will have something like a monthly cycle. A weekly one would be torment. An unfair burden.

Breathe, breathe. I must remember to breathe. It's all going to be fine. At least I'm not going to die a virgin. I've been desperate to get laid since I was seventeen and so very excited for my eighteenth birthday and my wedding. So much so that when my fiance had died in a car crash, my grief had been more for not getting railed, than for him. I am a terrible person. But I had barely known the man. I met him, what? Three times?

Anyway, I'm finally going to get what I've always wanted. A man, a mage, a husband. And he is a duke and not old or ugly. I should be grateful.

My head is pounding.

"May I be excused?" I ask.

"Of course, my dear," says Mother.

I nod at her and scurry away. Maybe lying down in a dark quiet room will stop me from disintegrating. I need to pull myself together. Everything I have ever dreamed of is about to happen. Wanting to sob hysterically is ridiculous.

My room doesn't feel comforting at all. Despondently I flop down onto my bed, still fully clothed.

It is going to be fine. Sothbridge is angry at me now, but I'm delightful. I will win him over. He will come to like me, I mean what's not to like? I'm cute, sweet. Desperate for cock. Any mage would be lucky to have me.

So what, if by everyone's best assessment I'm not going to be a very powerful vessel. They might be wrong, there is no way to really tell. Once I'm tapped I might burst with magic to give to my mage. And if not? Sothbridge is a very powerful mage. It's not like he needs any more magic.

As for my training? Well, it's a good thing my parents are progressive and haven't subjected me to that. I can hardly imagine that Sothbridge is a traditionalist. He is barely thirty for a start.

And, okay, my family is not the most prestiges or high-ranking, but he is a frigging duke. He doesn't need any help there either.

It's all fine. He won't hate me forever. He won't be an arrogant philanderer forever. I'll charm him. We will have a happy marriage and my family won't be ruined. Everything is great.

I roll over and bury my face in my pillows as giant sobs take over my body. I don't want anyone to hear me.

I may not be able to convince myself but I am sure as hell going to have everyone else believing it.

As far as the world is concerned, I'm delighted to be marrying Duke Sothbridge and I've never been happier.

Chapter Three

My sitting room has never been more sparkling clean, I'm sure of it. It looks like I'm ready to host the King, not a proctor. But I would probably be less nervous if I was meeting the King, apparently he is quite affable. Whereas Mr. Richards has a fearsome reputation and has scared me half to death, the few times I have met him.

The door bursts open and three of the staff struggle in carrying something heavy, and covered in a dust sheet, between them. Mr. Richards strolls behind them, dressed impeccably in a charcoal gray suit. He points imperiously towards the fireplace and the staff lug the thing over and place it where he directed.

Two more staff hurry in with smaller packages, and they lay them on the table.

Mr. Richards dismisses all the staff with a nod and then turns his steely gaze to me. I swallow convulsively.

"Good afternoon, Mr. Richards," I thankfully manage to say.

"Good afternoon, Master Witherington. I trust you know what this is?" he says as he gestures at the strange piece of furniture the staff just placed in front of my fireplace.

He strides over and whips off the dust sheet but the grand reveal doesn't help me at all. I still do not have the faintest clue what it could be. One glance at him confirms that my ignorance is plain to see.

I feel my cheeks flush as the weight of his disappointment settles on me. He is a trainer as well as a proctor. No doubt he is outraged that my parents never arranged for him or another trainer to instruct me in all the intricate and proper ways to be a vessel.

In his eyes, I should have started learning all of this on my sixteenth birthday. And here I am, twenty-one and clueless.

He is glaring at me expectantly, so I wander over to the item to see if I can figure it out.

It is a beautiful piece, whatever it is. It reminds me of a gym horse, but I doubt that is what it is. The wood on the legs and edges is dark mahogany. The body is covered in a deep red plush velvet. There is thick padding under the velvet and bright bronze rivets line the edge, where it meets the mahogany.

"Put your knees in there!" snaps Mr. Richards impatiently.

There are indeed two knee shaped holes cut into the body of the not-gym-horse-thing. Carefully, I do as I'm told. The padding is thick under my knees, it's surprisingly comfortable to kneel on. The holes are a little far apart so I'm having to spread my legs a little, but it's nothing unbearable.

"Now bend over and grasp the handles."

Okay. If I rest my stomach on the top of the not-gym-horse, I can reach down to the other side, where there are indeed handles.

"Hold your position," says Mr. Richards, from right behind me.

I nearly yelp in fright. He is standing in between my spread legs, and bent over like this, my ass is on full display. It feels like my trousers might as well be invisible.

"This is a rutting stool. It has been custom made to you and his grace's exact measurements, so when he stands behind you like so, you will be in a perfect position to receive him."

For the love of all things holy! I scramble off the thing as if it is made of lava, and practically knock Mr. Richards out of the way as I do so.

He glares at me but I am entirely too flustered to apologize.

"I am here to ensure you are prepared for your master, prudishness must be set aside," he declares haughtily.

He has a point. And I'm not a prude thank you very much. If anything, I'm the exact opposite of a prude. Or maybe I am in my head when I'm just thinking about carnal acts longingly. Perhaps when faced with the reality, I will shriek and faint like a blushing maiden. Gosh, that is a depressing thought.

Richards has walked over to the table, and he is now presenting me with one of the packages. Gingerly, I open it. Two inches of wood, wrapped around and around with strips of dark leather. The beautiful silver chain it is attached to, looks incongruous. The two parts quite simply do not go together.

"It's a brace!" I exclaim before he can snidely ask me if I know what it is.

I've never seen a new one before. Unmarked, unblemished. It's utterly spine chilling. The most terrifying thing I have ever seen.

"And what is it for?" Richards asks whilst raising an eyebrow. So much for thwarting his opportunity to be snide.

"You put it in your mouth and clench it between your teeth," I answer.

He nods. "Why?"

I swallow. "So you can bite down on it and stay quiet."

"Correct. Your master will not wish to be disturbed by your noise. A good vessel is a quiet vessel."

My heart is thrumming. Sothbridge isn't really into all of this, is he? He doesn't strike me as the sort. All this tradition stuff is just for show. When it is just the two of us, everything will be normal. Surely? He won't expect me to bend over that thing with this thing between my teeth while he rails me?

Images of the well-used braces I have seen, flow across my mind. Braces covered in indentations from teeth. A shudder convulses through my body. Plenty of people do still expect that. I have seen the evidence. Seen it worn around the necks of my patients.

I shove the brace into my pocket. I don't have to wear it around my neck like a nightmare-necklace until I'm married. Until then I'm just not going to think about it. Probably not the healthiest of coping mechanisms but it will have to do.

Richards gives me a small frown of disapproval but thankfully he says nothing. Instead, he merely turns and retrieves the next item. He presents the long, narrow box to me with a flourish, as if it is a bottle of fine champagne. I really, really don't want to open it. But I do.

Oh my. Instant regret floods through me. It's a dildo. In a very fancy red satin lined case, but still very much a dildo. It looks like clear glass and is exquisitely detailed, with veins and everything. I can't possibly look at Richards and my cheeks are on fire. I'm trapped here, staring at this thing.

"The phallus is an exact replica of your husband-to-be. So you may practice accommodating him."

A strange gurgling noise escapes from my throat. It feels like someone has taken a whisk to my brain. A replica? This detailed? This is wildly, wildly intimate. I feel like I should slam the lid shut so Richards stops staring at it. But there is another, far more pressing issue.

"It's um... scaled up?" I whisper hopefully.

"No. Exact replica."

My eyes are watering and I'm going to faint.

"Now, get undressed and on the bed. I will teach you how to prepare yourself to receive your husband."

My gaze flicks up to him in horror. The gleam in his eyes is positively evil. He pulls a bottle of lube out of his pocket and my heart stops.

"No! I... I mean, that's not necessary! I know how!"

He raises his eyebrow and gives me a thoroughly disparaging look. He knows I am a virgin. Everybody does. I'm a vessel. Having sex will change me forever and everybody will be able to tell. My innate magic will never be the same again.

"I'm a healer!" I explain. "I understand the... um physical side of things."

Richards's lip curls up in a sneer. "A duke consort with a trade? How vulgar."

Damn my flaming cheeks and damn Richards. "I am going to give it up, of course," I mumble.

Despite what Richards thinks, I know how to be proper. I'm going to be the best duke consort there ever was. If for no other reason than to spite everyone who thinks I can't do it.

Richards glares at me disapprovingly for a moment longer. Then slowly, ever so slowly he replaces the bottle of lube into his pocket. I swear I see a flash of disappointment in his eyes and it makes my skin crawl.

"I trust you know how to draw the seven ritual circles, for when your master requires your magic for a specific casting?"

My throat is too tight to swallow. I know a ritual circle is a collection of runes and symbols drawn on the floor in chalk or blood. And I know the vessel lies inside it while their mage takes them, but that's the extent of my knowledge. The burn of shame that flares through me hurts as I shake my head to admit my ignorance. Which was probably Richards's intent.

He sighs as if the weight of the world is upon his shoulders.

"It's going to be a long day."

I agree. A long, awful day.

He moves towards the bare floorboards by my window and pulls out a packet of chalk. But, hey, at least it is not lube.

Chapter Four

Finally, some peace and quiet. I'm all alone in my bed. My duties done for the day and all expectations drifting away. Why isn't everyone a night owl? The dark hours are so peaceful. There is no pressure to be doing anything in particular. The one part of the day where your time truly is your own. It's worth sacrificing a little sleep for.

Not that I'd be sleeping anyway. My mind is whirling. I'll never remember all the intricate circles Richards showed me. I can't learn in a day what usually takes two years to master. Sothbridge will just have to deal. He knows my family is progressive and that I have not received formal training.

His countless lovers would not have been trained. He doesn't seem to care about that. But I can't shake off this icy feeling of dread. And I don't think I'm being silly, because there is a huge difference between lovers and husbands, between dalliances and having your own vessel. He won't be taking me to bed for fun. He will have expectations.

Breathe, breathe. I must remember to breathe. There is no need to panic. I know the gist of it. Be quiet. Be biddable. Be submissive. How hard can it be? I should be able to do it. It's what I've always wanted for a start. My parents are more progressive than me. I want a husband. I want someone to be mage to my vessel. I want to host dinner parties and be charming. And I want to be railed regularly.

There are no lofty ambitions within me. No wistful yearning for freedom. I am happy with the role and destiny society has prescribed me. So why on earth am I being such a baby about it? Being quiet, biddable and submissive is a small price to pay, as much as the thought of it sinks my heart.

I need to concentrate on the positives. I'm gaining a husband. A duke no less. A young, handsome man. A well-endowed man. Now my cheeks are heating, I can feel it. Thank heavens there is no one to see.

My eyes treacherously flick to the box on my bedside table. There is no harm in having another look, surely? Scrambling to a sitting position in bed, my hands grab the box. I open the lid and gulp. Nope, I have not misremembered the size of it.

Depravity aside, it is a wonderful piece of craftsmanship. I run my finger along it. It's not hard and cold like glass, as I expected. It's warm and soft. A tingling quiver of magic itches up my hand. That's interesting. What is the magic for?

Alright, I can't resist anymore. I'm picking it up. It is definitely warm in my hand. I trace a finger from the base to the tip. Did it just twitch? I stare at it for a moment but nothing is happening.

Time to experiment. I wrap my fingers around it and start working it as if it were a real cock. And yes! It is growing warmer and it feels like it is swelling. So that's what the magic is for. What a wedding gift, a magical, responsive dildo!

I'm so glad there is no one here to hear my undignified snort laugh.

The dildo grows a little colder now that I've stopped fondling it and I almost feel bad for teasing it. As I stare at it some more, one thought starts to fill my mind. I wonder what it would feel like in my mouth?

I tried sucking off an ordinary toy once, and it was no fun at all, but this one will twitch and swell. It might even throb. It already feels warm and silken.

I stare at it. Sod it. Why the hell not? I'm alone in my bedchamber. And it's hardly as if I've never played with toys before. There is no need to be so nervous. Take a deep breath and begin.

Oh my goodness! It's only brushed past my lips and I can tell this is going to be amazing. The heat of it, the texture of it. It's weight. It is all divine and far better than any toy I have ever played with before. Sliding it over my tongue is heaven. It's definitely twitching too and heating up. It's a stretch to open my jaw wide enough. I wonder if I will ever have the real thing in my mouth?

Sex between a mage and vessel is supposed to be functional. The mage penetrates the vessel, brings them to orgasm which forces them to release their magic, which the mage then soaks up.

But Sothbridge is also to be my husband. The two do not necessarily go together, depending on the status of the vessel. But Sothbridge had to propose a marriage to avoid a scandal. What does that mean for our marriage? Will we do more than what is strictly between a mage and a vessel? Or will he forever be too furious at me to do more than tolerate my presence?

I don't want to think about that right now. I want to enjoy the feel of a cock in my mouth, even though it is fake. Though right now it's feeling very real. I just need someone to grab my hair.

I slide it in as far as I can go without gagging. It feels wonderful. Maybe with some practice I could learn how to take it deeper, but this is good for now. I bet a real one would smell incredible. All musky and masculine. That's something the spell casters forgot to add to their creation. Though this throbbing, and this heat is wonderful. I could suck on this forever. Run my tongue over every ridge and explore every part of it. Hum my pleasure.

Suddenly it moves in my mouth and in my hand. Far more than a twitch. Far more than it has before. It's pulsing. It's mimicking cumming. I want to giggle but a moan comes out of me instead. Gods, I sound filthy.

I feel a little breathless now and a lot horny. The only thought in my head is a longing to discover just how good this magic dildo is going to feel inside my ass. There is lube in my bedside cabinet. I'm not going to feel ashamed about reaching for it. I'm a grown man. I'm allowed to have fun. It might be my last chance to.

Chapter Five

Today is my wedding day. No matter how often I repeat the words in my head, they still don't feel real. I've drifted through the morning in a daze and it doesn't look like I am snapping out of this numb stupor anytime soon.

Mother hurries me into the car, and as we drive away I refuse to look back. I'm not looking back at my home, at everything I've ever known. The future is here and I'm going to have a new home, a new life. New roles and responsibilities. I really hope I don't faint.

The journey passes far too quickly and long before I am remotely emotionally prepared, we are sweeping up the driveway of Stourleat House. Duke Sothbridge's ancestral seat. I've seen it before, I've visited it numerous times on various social occasions but for some reason, today it looks enormous. Imposing. Daunting. Easily six times the size and grandeur of the home I have just left.

It belatedly, finally, fully strikes me that Sothbridge is a *duke*. I'm marrying a duke and all that entails. I'm going to be a duke consort. I knew this before, of course I did, but right now the reality of it is squeezing the air out of my lungs.

My father is an earl, not exactly low ranking, but very much not a duke. I have certainly achieved a climb up the social ladder. As I always intended to, so heavens know why I'm suddenly having the vapors about it.

Suddenly, we are right outside the house. Gleaming white stairs are curving up to the grand double doors. Staff are all lined up to greet us, to greet me as the new master of the house I suddenly realize. I swallow.

The door opens and I stumble out. Someone grabs my elbow and steadies me. The feel of the warm, firm touch sends a feeling like electricity coursing through my veins. I look up. It's him. It's Sothbridge. The look in his aquamarine eyes is intense. There is something in his look that wasn't there before, not the last time I saw him, anyway. The last time we met was in a dark maze and he had been nothing but furious. He doesn't look best pleased now. But there is *something*.

Awkwardly I smooth down my suit. I bet his isn't crumpled. I cast a quick glance to check. Nope. Impeccable. He is perfect. I mean his suit is perfect. Though I can not deny that the body filling it is exquisite. Such a shame about his personality.

He is taking me by the arm and leading me up the stairs. Time to concentrate on being all graceful and gracious. And I mustn't forget to smile.

He starts to introduce me to the staff. I really need to pay attention. These are the people who have the power to make my life hell if they don't like me. And I want them to like me anyway. I want everyone to like me. I adore most people so I don't see why the feeling shouldn't be returned. Plus, I am adorable. If only Sothbridge could see that.

Somehow I make my way through the greetings. The staff seem lovely. I can't discern any discontent. Perhaps Sothbridge isn't horrid to everyone. That's a promising sign.

Sothbridge whisks me along to the small, family chapel attached to the house. It is all gothic architecture and stained glass windows. I think it is lovely until I remember I'm about to get married in it. At least there is a small reprieve of meeting the guests.

I barely have time to set eyes upon Denise before she is wrapping her arms around me. Her stocky muscles haven't gotten any weaker, but she has grown out her salt and pepper buzz cut. This new pixie cut looks good on her.

"Good to see you, kid!"

"You too!" I grin. "How's the wife?"

"Beautiful," grins Denise.

I wish I could have wrangled a plus one for Denise but getting my former bodyguard invited was a feat in itself. As with most Old Blood weddings, there are only around thirty guests. Discreet, simple and humble is the aim.

"You did this on purpose, right?" she asks quietly so that only I will hear.

Her blue eyes are filled with concern and I feel awful. Time for my biggest grin. The one I reserve for emergencies.

"Of course!" I beam. "I planned to catch Sothbridge and it's all worked out perfectly!" My conspiratorial whisper sounds utterly believable.

She doesn't look entirely convinced, but she does know me, so I'm not surprised. She has witnessed firsthand the idiocy I am capable of.

"If you say so, kid. But if you need him kneecapped, just let me know."

I can't help giggling at the idea and when her expression softens, I'm glad. I really don't want her to think that her resignation to enjoy married life caused all this. Mother and I agreed to dally in hiring a replacement precisely to create the opportunity to ensnare Duke Rakeswell. I ended up catching Sothbridge instead, but hey, the plan 'marry a duke' has worked perfectly.

Denise flashes me another smile before going to find her seat. I look around the guests. So many people are missing. My older brother is still away on his top secret work. My cousin and good friend Eban has been cast out of society for having an affair with his bodyguard and causing his husband to divorce him in disgust. I don't even have any way of contacting him. I don't even know if he has heard that I am getting married. It's a little depressing. But it can't be helped. Yay for true love, I guess. At least I hope and assume he is living with Bastion in bliss somewhere.

Everyone falls silent. The priest has walked in. My heart is going to beat out of my chest, but by some miracle my legs are still working. I walk up to the altar and join Sothbridge.

The priest hurries through the marriage part. Everyone is far more interested in the joining of mage and vessel which comes next, but as he declares us wed, I can't fight the wave of sheer terror that washes over me at this irreversible thing that has been done.

My gaze flicks up to Sothbridge's. The priest places my hand into Sothbridge's warm, strong one and I'm sure the duke must feel me trembling. Sothbridge's striking eyes stare down at me, his pupils widen in surprise and then his look softens. He gives my hand a little squeeze as if he is trying to comfort me. Is he trying to be nice? This is wonderful. Maybe there is hope for us yet.

The priest raises his cowl and the chanting starts. A red cord is wrapped around our hands, symbolically joining us together. It's tied off in an elaborate knot, then everything stops. Everyone is staring at me. Oh gosh! Hastily I drop to my knees. How on earth did I forget this is the part where I kneel? I look up at Sothbridge who is towering above me. He places his unbound hand on the crown of my head, as he is supposed to, and he smirks. The bastard. Yes, okay, this is an extremely suggestive position but there is no need to be childish about it.

But the naughty gleam in his eyes is flipping my stomach over and the feel of his hand on my hair as I kneel here like this is stirring a lazy coil of desire within me. It's far too easy to imagine him curling his fingers into my hair, unzipping his fly and pulling me onto him. Memories of the weight and feel of the dildo flood my mind and suddenly I am very aroused. During my binding ceremony, in a chapel. On my wedding day. In front of friends and family. I'm such a fiend.

Luckily, it appears that when I'm truly mortified, I don't blush at all. At least I can't feel my cheeks heating. Perhaps I have drained of all color instead. Sothbridge certainly has something akin to concern in his eyes.

I stare back at him, and it is as if the rest of the world falls away. Nothing else exists save for this man. This man who is now my husband. My master. My mage. I can sense his powerful presence. I can feel the warmth of his body. His magic coils around me as if it is tasting me, exploring me. I feel like a mouse hypnotized by a snake but I'm not even sure if I want to escape.

My mouth stumbles over my vows. Especially the line about obeying. Thank heavens I rehearsed them so many times. My tongue is remembering even though my mind is not.

"Blessed be!" everyone chants, and it startles me.

It's done. That's the end of the ceremony. I am bound to Sothbridge. As his vessel and his husband. I think I am going to faint.

Chapter Six

It's my wedding night and I've been standing here staring at myself in the mirror for far too long. I'm clearly losing my mind. But when Sothbridge, *my husband,* finally makes it upstairs, I have to know if he is going to like what he sees.

The long white gown I'm wearing is traditional, so there is not a lot I can do about it. It fits me well, falling precisely to my ankles. It's sheer enough to be tantalizing without leaving me feeling too exposed.

My body is young and slender. It's covered in freckles but some people like that kind of thing, don't they? My hair is an interesting color, deepest auburn. It looks brown in some lights but it is definitely not. It's also very curly and I keep it just long enough to cover my ears, which are a little too big.

My eyes are large and brown, and my nose isn't crooked or anything. I'm not hideous to look at, by any means. But I have no idea what Sothbridge's type is. He said I was good looking at the ball, but he could have been just being a creep. What if he likes his men huge, hulking and hairy?

I let out a despondent sigh. At least he likes men. That's a good start. And it's going to have to do. Mages take vessels not of their sexual preference all the time. People want magic, not desirable bodies. So Sothbridge will desire my magic, if nothing else.

If he ever turns up. Vessels are supposed to retire first, to make the necessary preparations, which I have done. I've shoved so much lube up myself, I'm going to squelch when I walk.

I've also drunk the traditional tea. The recipe is a secret but my money is on it being a relaxant, aphrodisiac and mild sedative. I feel fine. The only effect I can place is that I'm only slightly nervous instead of outright terrified. Which is a good thing, I guess.

But I swear I left the celebrations an age ago. Surely Sothbridge should have joined me by now?

As if on cue, the door opens behind me and I whirl to face it. A wave of dizziness leaves me blind. Ah, okay, I guess the tea is having more of an effect than I thought. Suddenly Sothbridge is standing before me, the heat of his hands burning into my upper arms as he steadies me. All of a sudden I'm hyper aware of the giant bed a mere few steps away. As well as the rutting stool glowering in the corner.

"What's wrong with you now?" he sneers.

"Tea!" I splutter.

"Oh," he says and his gaze leaves my face to roam all over every inch of my body. I shudder.

I step back from him and attempt to regain some of my dignity. He is still staring at me intently.

"It was lovely to actually finish a formal dinner in peace," he remarks, inexplicably. "I had to leave the last one I attended early. Because you decided to play with the phallus."

His words bounce around my head without making any sense for a moment. The phallus? Is he talking about the magic dildo? How does he know I've played with it? That is mortifying. Slowly the true meaning of his words sink in. The dildo isn't imbued with magic to give a realistic experience. The magic connects it to his cock. It's like a voodoo doll. It's a voodoo cock. Everything that is done to it, he feels.

My hands are covering my mouth and I'm gasping in horror. I've been enjoying the magic dildo a lot. An awful lot. I've played with it every night since I was given it. It's been in my mouth and up my ass more times than I can count.

And he has felt it all.

Sothbridge chuckles. A deep, rumbling chuckle full of naughty promise. "I figured you didn't know."

"I... I... I'm so sorry!"

He grins. "It was fun."

I stare at him helplessly. What do I say to that? There are no words in the entire English language that can handle this.

"I thought having a virgin would be boring."

Indignation coils through me but it is a wispy, lazy thing. I'm too hopeful to be insulted. This is all going far better than I had expected. All it took was my utter mortification and humiliation. Look at me, accidentally seducing someone.

There is a fire in his eyes. He wants me. Hells, he has already felt what it is like to be inside me and he wants more. That is definitely flattering. I swallow dryly, still caught in his gaze. My cock is so hard it hurts but I have no idea if it's me or the tea. I have a feeling it is an unholy combination of the two.

"See, being married to me will not be all bad," I slur. Shit, this tea is really doing things to me.

He frowns, and the fire in his eyes fades. Damn it, I said the wrong thing. Too late now. It's not like I have a time machine. I can't take my words back.

"Your family is not good enough, your magic is not strong enough, you are not pretty enough, and you fucking ensnared me!"

I feel his words like the punches they are. They knock all the tentative hope out of me. He hates me. He is furious. We are stuck together forever in a loveless, resentful marriage. Maybe it's the tea, but I can see my long unhappy life spilling out before me. Stretching out forever in a cycle of never ending, misery filled days.

Tears fill my eyes and I can't stop them. Then a sniff escapes. Followed by a sob. Sothbridge's eyes widen.

"Oh for gods' sake, please don't cry!"

But I can't stop. It's like a damn has been unbroken. I'm crying. And not in a cute way. In a twisted-red-face-and-snot way.

I yelp in surprise as Sothbridge pulls me close. His arms wrap around me and my face is smooshed against his perfect pecs.

"I... I probably just needed to get that off my chest," he says awkwardly.

My sobs turn into wails. He meant every word. I know he did. My tears are just making him feel uncomfortable. Our society is very much stiff upper lip and not at all displays of emotion. He may have never seen anyone in this state before.

"Please stop crying." His voice is laced with desperation and anxiety.

Suddenly his hand is on my chin, pushing it away from his chest and pulling it up towards him. His lips touch my own and something zings along my entire body. My toes curl. Every part of me alights with fire. My head spins. I think every hair on my body is standing on end. My stomach flutters and my heart gives up.

Sothbridge is kissing me. His lips feel incredible. This cannot be happening. His arms are encircling my back. My body is pressing eagerly into his. I can feel the firm contours of his muscles. He is all masculine, blazing heat and divinity. He smells incredible. Like something I want to bottle and keep forever.

His tongue slips into my mouth, and I moan in delight. Surrendering to him completely. He can have every part of me that he desires. I am his.

He pulls away and I whimper at the loss. Reluctantly I open my eyes, to plead at him to continue. His aquamarine eyes are wide and hazy. He looks more shocked and surprised than I am, but he is the one who kissed me. Was he not expecting it to be that mind-blowing? At least, I hope it was mind-blowing for him too. Do kisses always feel like that?

I swear I felt that kiss in my very soul. But did he only mean to distract me from crying? It has certainly worked.

Now he is staring at me like he doesn't know what to do next. I hope he figures it out because I sure as hell don't have a clue.

"Do you know the names of the positions?" he asks.

I shake my head and drop his gaze so that I don't see his disappointment. I know there are, aptly, sixty-nine positions a vessel can assume for his master. They all have names like Ja-na-nie. Words from the Old Tongue that no one speaks anymore save for during incantations.

"You could show me?" I suggest.

I glance up just in time to see him frown.

"I mean, explain to me!" I correct hastily.

Heavens forbid he was thinking I was implying he should get himself into all sorts of undignified positions.

"How about you just lie on the bed for now?" he says.

"Umm... On my front?"

He shakes his head. "I want to see you."

His simple words give me goosebumps all over and sends my stomach into a full on cartwheel. My legs shake terribly as I make my way to the enormous bed. I want to climb onto it in a sultry, seductive manner, but all I manage is an undignified flop. I peer up at him through my eyelashes, he doesn't seem to mind about my lack of grace. Good.

I am finally, finally, at the grand old age of twenty-one, about to lose my virginity. In my opinion, it's not a moment too soon. I've been waiting for this moment since puberty got its claws into me. If I hadn't been born a vessel, and was free to do as I chose, I'm pretty sure I would have worked my way through Grindr by now. So Sothbridge may be an arrogant asshole, but he is a good-looking one, and he is here and I'm not going to complain.

He walks over to the bed and I can feel the weight of his gaze burning into me. He stops, but does not climb onto the bed. Instead, he continues to stare at me.

"I want to see if those freckles are all over," he says and his voice sounds thick and husky.

I nod. I'm a long way from words right now.

His fingers curl into the hem of my nightgown. I look away as he slides it up my body, baring me to him. He reaches my waist so I lift up my hips a little so he can continue. He drags the cloth up and up until the white gauze is bunched around my neck and I am utterly naked before him.

He licks his lips, and his eyes darken. I shiver. I think he likes what he sees.

"May I touch you?" he whispers.

I nod again. He is my husband. My master. He doesn't need to ask. But I like that he has.

His fingers brush along my chest. A soft caress along my bare skin. It feels like he leaves a trail of fire. His touch drifts down and down, across my stomach and lower still. His hand dances feather-soft on my aching cock. I moan. No one has ever touched me there before and it feels like heaven. I want more of this, I want all of this. I want this to never end.

He moves around to the foot of the bed. His hands grab my hips and suddenly he is sliding me down across the sheets, to the very edge of the bed. I yelp in surprise. Then I stare in bewilderment as he drops to his knees. My mouth drops open to say something, but his mouth descends onto my cock and the world explodes with sensation. There is nothing but the hot wet heat of his mouth. My back arches, my fingers clutch at the sheets, my head tilts back and a truly filthy noise escapes my throat.

He is merciless. He lavishes my cock with divine attention until I'm squirming and panting. Sparks of pleasure are dancing all over my body. I have never felt anything like this. I'm gasping, I can't breathe but I don't want this to ever stop. I have never felt more alive.

"Soth... Sothbridge!" I moan.

He releases my cock with a soft plop, and I whine in dismay.

"For heaven's sake. Call me Harry when I'm sucking your cock."

"O... O... Okay." I burble in reply.

He chuckles and then devours me again. The shriek that erupts out of me is not at all dignified but the sudden assault of renewed pleasure is setting fireworks off in my brain. My balls are drawing up and I'm tingling all over. My legs are trembling as if they have a mind of their own.

"Soth... Ha... Harry!"

He is paying me no heed and I'm about to blow. Right in his mouth. Frantically I grab his hair and pull him off. I suck in a desperate breath. I'm shaking all over and still feel like I'm a hair's breadth away from erupting.

"Ow," says Harry as he rubs his scalp.

"Sorry! I didn't want to... in your..."

He flashes me a truly devilish grin. It looks like he wouldn't have minded that at all. But it wouldn't have been proper. He is my master. It is our wedding night. He is supposed to be tapping me. He needs to make me come while he is inside me. That is what will release my magic. And once it discovers sex brings it freedom, my magic will drive my body to seek it regularly. Either every seven days or monthly. Or whatever rhythm my magic settles into.

"You think I can't make you come more than once?" he drawls in a teasing pur.

A strange noise is the only thing that comes out of my mouth in reply. He chuckles again before sliding me back up the bed. He strips his clothes off and joins me without giving me a chance to appreciate the view.

But now he is lying naked on top of me, and this is far better. I don't remember spreading my legs, but they are very, very spread. I'm so debauched and wanton. And it seems he has decided to get on with the main event.

His fingers trace around my well lubed hole. A low groan rumbles out of him. I think he likes that I prepared myself well for him.

He shifts position and something is pushing at my entrance, something that is very much not fingers. Oh gods, this is it. The very tip of him eases inside me and I'm transported to heaven on a wave of ecstasy. This feels incredible. Far better than the magic dildo. The real thing is both firmer, softer, as well as hotter. It feels like silk and I want all of it. I want it to stretch me wide and fill me deep. I want Sothbridge, I mean Harry, inside me. I want him to take me and make me his.

Slowly, so slowly it is almost torture, he inches inside me and gives me everything I am craving.

Reality melts away. I'm flying, soaring through a sky made of bliss, pleasure and sheer euphoria. Harry is all around me, inside not only my body, but also my soul. How is it possible to be so entwined with another person? I can't tell where I end and he begins. We are one.

My body is writhing in carnal delight but I'm exulting in something far deeper. Is it always like this or is it our magic singing in harmony? I guess I will never know. He is the first man I have surrendered my body to and he will be my last. He is my husband, my master, my mage. That is sacred.

"Sothbridge!" I wail in delight.

"I told you to call me Harry," he grunts.

"When you are sucking my cock," I manage to reply.

He chuckles without slowing his pace. "Just call me Harry, I'm your flipping husband."

I moan something that I hope gives an affirmative impression. I'm not capable of being anymore coherent right now.

He is thrusting into me now. My hips are rising up to meet him eagerly. My orgasm is already building, coiling and twisting within me, gathering power like a storm that is about to be unleashed.

And suddenly it is freed. It tears through my body, my mind, my soul. My magic. I am undone. Unraveled. Every part of me blown apart and scattered upon waves of ecstasy. I cry out and am carried far, far away.

Chapter Seven

Slowly consciousness calls me back, I drift back to it languidly but I'm feeling a sense of unease. I open my eyes to find the pale pre-dawn sky softly illuminating my new bedchamber.

I'm cold. Alone. My bed is empty. Harry has left.

My body is aching to be held. And it is also just aching. I feel well used. My magic feels strange. I feel hollow. It's all rather unsettling. I have definitely been changed. I am different now. No longer an untapped vessel. No longer a virgin.

I grab a pillow and hug it to me like it is a teddy bear. A sniff confirms there is no trace of Harry on it. I doubt he even rested his head on it. He probably left as soon as he was done. But I can't stop clinging onto this pillow.

It's fine that he left. It's proper. We are not lovers. We are vessel and mage. Duke and duke consort. We do not share a bed or rooms.

The pillow is getting wet from my tears and I didn't even realize that I was crying. I'm being ridiculous. My wedding night went far better than I had any right to hope for. He wasn't cruel or disinterested, despite having every right to be. He gave me a blow job for heaven's sake, I know enough to know that's rare for a mage to do for his vessel. I'm very lucky and I should be grateful.

And sex is every bit as amazing as I suspected it was, and now I no longer have to go without. Harry will be coming to my bed regularly. I hope my cycle ends up being weekly. That will be a whole lot more fun than monthly. A strange giggle escapes from me. Oh dear, I sound hysterical. It's a good thing there is no one here to hear.

I lie alone in my bed, watching the sky lighten and the sunrise, until it is time for breakfast. Then I shower and dress before heading with some trepidation to the breakfast room. Is Harry going to be there? What kind of greeting will I receive?

Taking a deep breath, I open the door and enter. Harry is sitting at the table reading a newspaper with a cup of black coffee in front of him. The winter morning light is streaming through the window and illuminating his golden hair. He looks gorgeous. I can sense his power and it is laced with magic that used to be my own. It makes me feel a little queasy.

Aquamarine eyes glance up from his paper to meet my gaze. He nods in greeting and turns his attention back to reading.

Okay, that wasn't hostile at least. But it wasn't exactly warm. I stumble over to the serving table and grab a croissant and an orange juice, mostly for something to do. Should I sit next to him? No, that is far too forward. I'll take a seat across from him instead.

We sit in silence. Is it comfortable silence? I hope so. Should I say something? I'll just pour myself a cup of tea for now.

I'm startled by a young man strolling into the breakfast room. The first thing I see is his legs that seem to stretch forever. He is wearing tiny tight pink shorts so there is plenty of perfect pale leg to see. He is also wearing a glittery sequin bestrewn crop top, so there is also a lot of perfect stomach and midriff to see. His long dark hair tumbles in gorgeous soft waves past his shoulders.

He strides up to the serving table, grabs a pastry and shoves it in his mouth. He is beautiful and exotic. Is he Harry's lover? I swallow. Now I feel all kinds of inadequate.

"Jem, please tell me that you did not just get in," says Harry, sounding awfully exasperated.

Jem shrugs. "Fine. I won't tell you that. I'll tell you that I spent the night curled up in my own bed with a mug of coco."

He nonchalantly takes a seat and places his bare feet up on the table. His toenails are painted with rainbow glittery polish.

"Jem!" growls Harry.

Jem rolls his eyes and removes his feet from the table before taking another huge bite of the pastry. Harry continues to glare at him until eventually the young man surrenders.

"Don't worry, I didn't give anyone the goods. My magic is untouched. All nice and ready for the next mage who wants it."

I thought he was a vessel! And if the tingling of my skin is anything to go by, he is a very powerful one too. This is awful. I can't compete with him! He is a ten to my three, and that's me being generous to myself. I need to sip my tea to cover my face and hide my expression.

"Good," says Harry, sounding very relieved.

"I just sucked a lot of cocks instead."

I splutter my tea everywhere, and Harry's face darkens. Jem smirks at us both, looking entirely too pleased with himself.

"What? What's going to happen? I'm going to be shamed and ostracized from society?" He clutches at his heart in mock fear. "Oh… wait… that's already happened." He shoves the remainder of the pastry into his mouth rather aggressively.

Harry sighs wearily.

My gaze flicks between the two of them. I'm not sure what to do or say, or where to look.

"Colby, this is my brother, James Cambell. Jem, this is my husband and vessel, Colby," Harry says drolly.

Jem leans back in his chair, snatches another pastry off the serving table and raises an eyebrow at me. "Oh, sorry. I assumed you were just his latest conquest."

"Jem!" Harry yells and smashes his fist against the table but Jem doesn't even flinch.

Instead, he puts on an innocent face. "Oh goodness, was the wedding yesterday? I guess I forgot, probably because I wasn't invited."

"Jem! Fuck off!" snarls Harry.

Jem huffs, rolls his eyes and flounces out of the breakfast room whilst still eating his second pastry.

Harry turns to me, and he looks rather deflated. "Sorry about him," he mutters.

"It's fine," I smile.

And it really is. I'm just hugely relieved that Jem is his brother and not his sexy and powerful lover. Though the news that Harry has an obviously tapped, yet unbonded hellion of a vessel as a brother is a little alarming. I vaguely recall hearing that

Harry had a younger brother and that he was sickly. I love gossip. I thrive on it. How on earth have I not heard about Jem?

Harry has done a fantastic job in keeping the black sheep of the family a secret. Which makes me wonder, what else is he hiding?

I watch Harry as he turns back to his newspaper, but his secrets are not suddenly laid bare for me to see. It's unsettling, but I'm sure it is fine. Everyone has secrets. Especially wealthy, powerful men. Harry may not be the nicest person but I really don't think he is going to hurt me or cause me any harm. Neglect and ignore, yes. Actual malice? No. So therefore his secrets are none of my business.

And he didn't like Jem being rude to me. That has to be a good sign? A sign that I'm safe at least. Harry is going to protect me, even if for no other reason that I am his husband and any insult to me, is an insult to him. I have nothing to worry about.

"So, what are our plans for today?" I ask brightly.

Harry puts his paper down. "Your time is your own. I have no need of you until you are ripe."

Oh. Okay. I gulp my orange juice in an effort to hide my crushed expression. It's entirely my own fault for expecting too much. My glass is empty and I have to put it down, but my eyes are still watery.

Abruptly, Harry stands up. "Let me know when you are ripe," he says, and he strolls away, out of the room.

I blink and stare after him. I think I will know when I'm ripe. I've never experienced it before, but I get the impression it is hard to miss. My magic will brim and I will be unbearably horny. It could happen tomorrow, or in a month. It will be sporadic and all over the place until it settles into a rhythm. Terribly inconvenient for Harry. He will need to stay near me so he can empty me when it happens, so I don't explode or burn his house down or something.

He is a busy man who usually travels around the world for business and now he is tethered here to me until my rhythm is established and he can plan his calendar around me. I swallow tightly. I've exploded into his life and disrupted everything, when the only thing he did was be in the wrong place at the wrong time.

I need to make it up to him somehow. I need to be the best vessel and husband there ever was. And that means, I need to go find the housekeeper. My parents didn't want to subject me to vessel training, but they taught me how to run a large house efficiently. I'm sure Harry's housekeeper is competent, but it is my duty as consort to oversee everything. There may be some things I can improve on.

With a renewed sense of purpose, I hurry from the room. First day of the rest of my life.

Chapter Eight

I leave my meeting with Mrs. Matterson, the housekeeper, feeling rather deflated. She is a formidable woman, that is for sure. It's going to take a while to win her over with my charm and help her to see that I'm not threatening her job, I'm here to make it easier. I can be an asset.

Oh well, time is one thing I don't have in short supply. Like right now. What on earth am I going to do with myself? Languishing in my rooms doesn't sound fun at all. Looking around the hallway I'm walking down doesn't give me any inspiration. Oh! I know! I could explore the house. There are bound to be parts that weren't included in my grand tour and those probably are the bits I really need to see. Neglected rooms. Leaky corners. Sections the staff don't dust because no one ever checks.

Humming to myself I set off on my new adventure. It feels good to have a direction and a purpose. Something to do that I'm actually good at.

A few hours later, I'm covered in dust. I have a lot of notes on my phone of repairs that need doing and rooms that need a thorough clean out. I open another door and freeze in surprise. This room isn't dusty and neglected like the rest of this wing.

This room is well used. And full of magical paraphernalia. It's a ritual room.

My gaze takes in the crystals, dried herbs, and the runes marked on the walls. It takes me a moment to identify the type of arcane lore I'm looking at. As soon as I do, I swallow uneasily. My husband is a Revivalist. Or as my parents call them, idiots.

I kind of agree with my mother and father. Why anyone would want to bring the fey back to our realm is beyond me. By all accounts the fey were ruthless, cold, vicious and murderous. Whether or not they are our distant ancestors and regardless if they are the reason we have magic, I'm pretty sure they would show us no mercy if someone did succeed in bringing the fey realm close enough for portals to work again.

They'd probably just take over the world and subjugate all humans. Not caring if we are Old Blood or mundane. I shiver.

The idea that I have magic because my great, great, great something shagged a fey, is unsettling and I've never been able to believe it. I don't know why some humans have magic and most do not, but that explanation just seems so fanciful. Though clearly, magic is hereditary. Hence why all the noble families are fanatical about breeding.

I huff out a breath. I'm just a vessel. All these theological questions are far above me. I just need to make sure not to ever voice my opinions, so I don't insult my husband. It should be easy enough to do. It's not as if the topic of conversation comes up very often. It's far too divisive to be considered a polite subject.

I shiver again. What is wrong with me? Am I getting sick? Oh gosh, I can't possibly be ripe already? Something that feels a lot like dread clutches my stomach. Frantically, I assess myself. No, I'm not full of magic. In fact, I'm fairly empty. Which makes sense, I was taken last night. As my slightly sore ass can confirm.

But there is an awful lot of magic swirling around me. Thick and potent. Raw, natural earth energy, just seeping out of the ground. Oh wow. All the noble houses were built on such naturally occurring wells. Sadly, my family's one dried up a hundred years ago. But it seems this one is still going strong. Very strong.

I've been to Stourleat House before. Balls and dinner parties. But I never felt this before. Come to think of it. I didn't feel it yesterday or last night. It must be shielded. Hidden. That makes sense. Harry wouldn't want anyone to know how much power he has access to. People would want it. People would plot to murder him and his family and get their hands on Stourleat House and its huge well of magic.

I swallow nervously. Another thing I'm going to have to pretend not to know. This exploration plan was terrible.

A sudden thought makes me nearly heave. What if Harry thinks I already knew? What if he believes this is why I trapped him into marriage? Oh gosh, I'm going to faint. He would loathe and despise me if that were the case.

But surely anyone can see I'm harmless? A bit dim? I'm definitely not a cunning schemer hungry for power. A chess piece in a plot against him. Unless he thinks my entire personality is just an act. Oh my. How on earth am I going to convince him that I really am just dumb and ensnaring him in marriage was a genuine accident?

My feet are fleeing and returning to safer parts of the house. It's a great idea. At least some part of me is capable of competence.

I reach the relative safety of my room and try to remember how to breathe. It's all good. Harry hasn't been cruel to me so far, so he can't believe that. Or he is at least giving me the benefit of doubt. I just need to give him no reason to suspect anything. Except now, I'm just going to look as guilty as hell whenever I'm with him.

Oh well, he doesn't seem to want my company. As he made perfectly clear at breakfast. So it's all worked out for the best.

Deep breath. Calm down. It's all going to be fine. Just no more exploring! Mind my own business. Stay out of trouble. Don't be a nuisance. I can do that. I will do that. I'm still determined to be a fabulous consort. I'm going to be so amazing, that one day Harry won't regret that he had to marry me.

And then, everything will be wonderful.

Chapter Nine

This spreadsheet is starting to not make any sense. Maybe I should take a break, but I am so very nearly done. Just a little longer. If I leave it now, I'll be in a right muddle when I try to pick it up again.

"Colby," says someone from the doorway of the library.

"Hmm?" I answer.

Looking up, I am startled to see night has fallen. The only light in here is from the computer screen. I'm also surprised to see that it is Harry striding towards me. I haven't seen him for three days. Since breakfast on the morning after our wedding. Not that I have been counting or anything.

"What are you doing?" he asks.

"Oh, Just going over the accounts!" I explain. "Did you realize that the head gardener is willing to take a cut in his salary in exchange for accommodation? And the gatehouse is empty, which is costing a small fortune in maintenance. So two birds, one stone!" I beam at him happily.

He just stares at me. An unfathomable expression on his face. He doesn't look impressed at all. I try to hide my disappointment and start shutting down all my tabs so I can be an attentive husband.

"You are ripe."

"Oh!" I glance back up at him in surprise.

Am I? A quick assessment confirms that I am indeed brimming with magic. And I'm feeling very light-headed and a little sweaty. My jaw drops open in surprise. How could I have not noticed? And now Harry has had to come and find me. Probably after sensing me hours ago and wondering why I wasn't coming to him. This is so embarrassing.

"You didn't know?" asks Harry and the suspicious gleam in his eyes makes my stomach churn uncomfortably.

I can only shake my head and hope that he believes me.

He frowns a little and my heart sinks.

"Come on then," he says, tilting his head towards the door.

My body starts to shake. I can feel my heartbeat in my throat. Why am I so nervous? Sex is fun. There is nothing to worry about. I give Harry a big smile as I walk around the desk and up to him. A strange look flashes across his face. He grabs my elbow and I realize that I have stumbled. He must think I'm so clumsy. I'm always stumbling in his presence.

He doesn't let go of me as he takes me back to my bedchamber. He sits me on the bed and kneels before me to untie my laces and take my shoes off. He is undressing me but this doesn't feel the least bit sexy. It's like he is helping an invalid.

He pushes me back until I am lying on the bed, so he can work my trousers and underwear off. I wonder if he will leave my shirt on, as he only needs access to my lower half. I'm about to giggle, when he starts unbuttoning my shirt and something about his deft fingers moving so close to my skin, grabs my full attention.

I'm half naked but I don't feel shy. Can't blame anything on tea this time, but I suppose I can blame being ripe. It is supposed to make vessels feel out of sorts.

"Oh no!" I exclaim.

Harry pauses and gives me a quizzical look.

"I haven't prepared... down there!" I whisper while pointing at my nether regions, as if Harry needs help in understanding what I'm on about.

His bright eyes flash and he shakes his head as if he can't quite believe how daft I am. But there is also a faint smile on his lips.

"It's fine," he says, and I love the deep rumble of his voice.

He finishes undoing my shirt, then he walks over to the bedside cabinet and retrieves a bottle of lube. And my brace. He hands it to me without meeting my gaze. I take it with numb fingers. I didn't use it on our wedding night. Does this mean he wants to do this formally? Because our first time wasn't formal at all. Anxiety claws at me. I don't really know how to have sex ritually. Like a vessel and mage should. I only know that I'm supposed to be quiet and submissive. If he wants anything more, he is going to have to teach me.

The slurp of the lube bottle makes me cringe. Not the most romantic of sounds. He kneels on the bed next to me, still fully clothed. It's kind of hot.

"Would you mind?" he asks.

"Oh! Of course!" I reply as I hurriedly spread my legs wide.

His slick fingers trace around my hole and his touch is like electricity, shooting pleasure and sensation all along every nerve ending in my body. I can feel his magic calling to mine, like a siren song. Alluring, enticing. Dangerous. No, not dangerous. What is wrong with me? I'm not in any peril. There is no need to freak out. Giving him my magic is a good thing. It's not as if I can wield it. It is of no use to me. Surrendering it to him is my fundamental duty as a vessel.

And I get a whole ton of pleasure as a reward. This is good. This is wonderful. It is everything I have ever wanted. Harry may not have been my first choice, but everything is fine.

He slowly eases a finger inside me. The gentle stretch makes me gasp. It feels so good. I love having something in there. He hasn't touched my cock but I don't care. I'm so very aroused that I'd probably blow even if he accidentally brushed it. This is better. He needs to be inside me when I come so he can take my magic.

My gaze accidentally finds his, and he is watching me intently. As if he is drinking in my reactions, my every gasp, squirm and moan. His eyes are wide and dark with lust. That look seems to bore into my very soul and ignite a fire inside me. He is ridiculously handsome, and he wants me. I groan as a fresh wave of pleasure consumes me.

He adds a second finger and finds my prostate. I cry out and clutch at the sheets. His fingers stroke and tease and I'm writhing and bucking and helpless before him. He is damn good at this.

"Ha... Harry!" I wail.

I'm seeing stars. I'm about to spill and he is not inside me yet. Mercifully, the fingers disappear, to be replaced by the pressure of his cock demanding entry. I groan, it feels good but also uncomfortable. He is not small. He pushes relentlessly in, forcing my body to open for him. I gasp.

Suddenly he is shoving the brace into my mouth. Startled, I accept it.

"A good vessel is a quiet vessel," he grunts as he continues to work his way inside me.

I bite down on the brace as my back arches. He is all the way in now and I'm stretched very, very wide and filled very, very deep. It feels incredible but intense. A little overwhelming.

Gently he starts to roll his hips, and I am grateful for his care. Lust and pleasure swell within me, taking away the discomfort and leaving only bliss. I whimper into my brace.

My whole body is alight. My orgasm is building and building. He slides in and out. In and out. Each movement rubbing delicious friction and joy into me until it crests and I'm bucking and clenching around him, biting down on the brace as hard as I can while a scream reverberates in my throat. My magic surges out of me and into him as my orgasm tears through me.

The moment stretches. Suspended in time, then snaps like an elastic band. Leaving me spent and boneless on the bed. My chest is heaving. My head is spinning. Echoes of intense pleasure are tingling and sparking all over my body.

I hear the sound of Harry's fly and open my eyes just in time to see him turn around and walk out without a word. Leaving me sprawled and naked and used on the bed.

I clench my eyes tightly shut to trap the tears. I'm not going to cry. I'm not. I'm going to bite down on this brace and hold back my sobs. Everything is fine. He is treating me exactly as a mage should treat his vessel.

I have nothing to be upset about.

Chapter Ten

It's Mrs. Matterson's day off, so I'm going to seize this opportunity to inspect the linen closet. It's not that I'm scared of her. It's me being diplomatic and not ruffling any feathers. This way she will never know, and I'll get the distraction I need. Everyone gets to be happy.

As I make my way down the hallway, I can't help anxiously checking my magic. Harry emptied me and left me alone on the bed two days ago, there is no way I could be ripe again. But I can't help checking. It's turning into a compulsion.

My magic stirs lazily at my metaphorical touch. There is far more of it than I would expect after only two days, but I'm nowhere near full. A wave of relief washes over me and I am ashamed by it. I should want to give my mage my magic, it is my duty.

I open the door of the linen closet and squeak in surprise. There is a young man in here. He is wearing faded jeans and a plain blue tee shirt. His dark hair is tied up in a neat bun and there is a pen tucked behind his ear. A clipboard is in one hand and he is rummaging in the linens with the other. He turns to face my intrusion and his aquamarine eyes flash with resigned disappointment.

It's Jem. Harry's brother. An unwed vessel. Of course he is going to be keeping an eye on his family's home. Why didn't Mrs. Matterson say? She could have told me I was superfluous. Unneeded. Useless.

"Oh, my apologies, I didn't realize that you were taking care of things," I hear myself say.

Jem flashes me a sad look and shrugs. "It was something to do."

I open my mouth to say something and leave him to it, but he surprises me by handing me the clipboard. Then he takes the pen out from behind his ear and hands it to me as well.

"You're the master of the house now. Duke Consort Sothbridge. It is your role."

"No, it's fine. I'm sure you are doing a grand job."

Jem shakes his head. "Harry was always going to get married one day. Besides, I'm bored of doing it."

His tone is flippant but his eyes are still sad. I'm trying to think of what to say or do, when he brushes past me and starts walking away.

"Jem!"

He stops and turns back to face me.

"Oh gosh!" I gush. "May I call you Jem?"

He gives me a rueful smile, "Please do, if you call me James, I'll think I'm in awful trouble."

I smile back at him. He seems nice. And he clearly needs to feel useful too. I can't take away his occupation and leave him with nothing to do. That would be beyond cruel.

"Were you formally trained as a vessel?" I blurt.

His eyes cloud with suspicion and I have never seen anyone look more wary, but he nods.

"You have probably heard that I wasn't." I stop and blush. "I could do with some tips."

Guilt niggles at me for betraying my progressive values, but I hate being ignorant. Besides, knowing what Harry expects from me, doesn't mean I'm necessarily going to do it. It merely means I will understand the situation better.

His eyebrows raise in surprise, and he crosses his arms. He doesn't say anything for a long moment. Then he finally speaks.

"You want me to teach you how to be a good vessel?" he says, sounding both incredulous and mocking at the same time.

"You've been trained," I answer with a shrug. It really is quite straightforward, I can't understand his strange reaction to my request.

"I seduced my trainer," he says slowly and carefully. As if he thinks I am daft.

I gasp in horror. Oh my goodness! That was what got him ostracized from society! This is awful. A thousand thoughts and images crowd my mind as everything clicks into place like a jigsaw puzzle being revealed.

"I know? Very shocking isn't it?" he says drolly, but I can see the defensiveness in every line of his body.

"No! I mean, yes, but not you!" I hurry to explain. "Your trainer was an adult, it was his profession, and you were what seventeen?" I ask hopefully, but his face is blank. Since vessel training starts on your sixteenth birthday and ends when you are wed at eighteen. I'm really hoping his abuse happened towards the end of his training. "Sixteen?" I add even though I really don't want to. Jem's answering flush makes my stomach heave.

"Mr. Richards has never put a foot wrong before or since," Jem says stonily.

I shudder. I should have guessed it was that horrid man. The look in his eyes when he wanted to teach me how to open myself up, will haunt me forever.

"Mr. Richards is a creep. My cousin Eban had him and I saw how he was changed," I say, cowardly backing out of sharing my own experience.

Jem looks entirely unconvinced and I'm momentarily distracted by how very pretty he is. We are around the same age but he has a grace and a refinement that I will never achieve. It makes me feel wistful. I shake my head to clear from such shallow thoughts. He is sharing his awful past with me and I'm getting jealous over his looks.

"Anyway, all trainers are creeps." I continue. "What kind of men choose a career where they move in with a teenager and spend two years teaching them sixty-nine different ways to bend over and take it?" I exclaim in disgust.

I've never been more grateful that my parents saw sense and chose not to subject me to that. It's terrifying to think that Jem's fate could have so easily been my own.

Jem's eyes narrow. "Well, I was having so much fun with a dildo, making such filthy noises and arching my back so prettily that he couldn't resist taking the dildo out and replacing it with the real thing."

He is trying to shock me. It's his shield and his weapon. The way he defends himself. But I'm not so easily shocked, not when it comes to matters like this. I'm a healer. I mean, I was a healer. I may have given it up now that I'm married, but my knowledge remains. I may look clueless but I'm not naïve. I know how the world works and I know how cruel dirty old men can be.

"If you stimulate the prostate correctly, anyone who has one is going to become very aroused. It's biology, not a character flaw," I announce with determination.

He is staring at me openmouthed now, and my heart is breaking. He has been taught to really, truly believe it was all his fault. And it is so clear that he has taken that lesson to heart and embraced it.

"And I'm willing to bet good money he has done it to lots of his victims, his so-called trainees," I add ruthlessly. Jem has to be shown the truth. I can't let him fester in this undeserved guilt anymore, the injustice of it is scalding my soul.

Jem looks incredulous.

Hurriedly I continue my explanation. "I bet he normally withdraws in time. Makes his victim think it was all their fault and graciously agrees to never tell a soul. But with you, he misjudged, and he accidentally tapped you."

Jem's eyes are huge.

"It wasn't your fault," I state calmly, clearly. I want these four words to sink into his very soul and become a part of him forever.

Silence falls. The hallway probably wasn't the best place for this conversation but it can't be helped now. Jem is shock still, staring at me as if I have just upended his world. Good. I hope I have. I'm shaking with fury at everyone who has done this to him, everyone who told him he was to blame for his abuse. How could Harry do this to his brother? His younger brother, who he is supposed to protect and care for?

Poor, poor Jem. He was raped when he was sixteen and banned from society for it. He will never be wed. Never be loved. He will be alone forever. He is a vessel so he can't settle down with a mundane, he needs a mage to empty him, and I can't even bear to think about how that need is being dealt with. But from what I know of society, and Jem's comment at breakfast about his magic being ready for whichever mage wants it, I have a horrid suspicion that he is pimped out whenever he is ripe.

The whole situation is horrendous and heartbreaking. And I'm so furious at Harry, I think I might explode.

Jem silently turns on his heels and flees. I don't mind at all. I really hope he thinks about what I have said and doesn't just dismiss my words entirely. I could have been more tactful, but I was just so enraged that I couldn't hold it in.

I sigh and try to calm down. But it's not working. Realization of what I have just done is slowly starting to sink in. I wanted to be an unobtrusive husband. I didn't want to disrupt anything. My plan was to get Harry to forgive me for tricking him into marriage by giving him no cause for concern.

But now I've gone and exploded like a firework with my thoughts and opinions. And what is worse is that I'm pretty certain that next time I see Harry, I will not be able to keep my mouth shut.

What on earth am I going to do?

Chapter Eleven

Harry

Colby is in the library, I can sense the beautiful song of his magic. I want to go talk to him, but here I am pacing my sitting room and hiding like a child. It's ridiculous. I only want to ask him if he would like to have dinner with me in my rooms.

I want to ask my husband to dine with me. I should not be feeling so daunted by this simple thing. But then again, none of my reactions make sense when it comes to Colby. That young man has well and truly gotten under my skin.

I need to check my files again. It's stupid because I have read them a thousand times. I sigh, maybe one last time will finally reassure me. I reach into my pocket and pull out my phone. My fingers know the route to his file well. All the information I could find out about him. Everything I had my people dig out.

I scan the pages again. His family are not Revivalist nor part of any active Anti groups. And he is not connected to anyone who is likely to know how much raw power lies here at Stourleat. Colby is no threat at all.

The only dirt that could be found on him, was that he was somehow involved in aiding his cousin Lord Eban du Fray runaway with his bodyguard. I sigh. Gorgeous, flirtatious Eban. I miss seeing him at various functions. Especially since his husband had been very willing to share his vessel. My stomach twists uncomfortably. Now that I have had Colby in my arms, Eban's reluctance seems obvious. And that makes me think of all the vessels that have been shared with me over the years.

My feet take me over to the drinks cabinet, and I pour a whiskey. Memories of being in Colby's bed taunt me. He was so eager, sincere. *Willing.* He wanted me, enjoyed me.

I down the whiskey in one swift move. I know I live in a dark, twisted world. I know I'm not a good person. But Colby's sweet innocence is shining a light on all my failings and it's damn uncomfortable.

I quickly scan the rest of the file. His family have hit financial hardship. That's it. The incident in the maze was as innocuous as that. No grand plan. No devious scheme. It's refreshing.

And now I have a sweet, innocent and fundamentally good person in my life. He doesn't belong here. I don't deserve him, and I certainly don't want to drag him down into my darkness. Tarnish him with my touch. If I was a good person, I'd leave him alone as much as possible and let him continue to burn brightly.

But I'm not a good person. As much as Colby makes me want to be one. I crave his light. I want to stand blinking before it. Dazzled and uncertain. I yearn for it like a starving man for food. It's as if I think Colby can save me, lead me back to the light after a lifetime of treading a path of darkness.

With that thought, suddenly I am striding towards the library. I'm being ridiculous. Colby can't save me. No one can. All that is going to happen is that I'm going to harm him. I wince. I hurt him last time I took him. His pain laced whimpers and his flash of uncertainty had been like daggers shredding my soul. And all I had done was to shove his brace in his mouth so I didn't have to hear him. I am a monster. I should turn around right now. But I can't. I'm not strong enough. I'm like a moth to his flame, except he is the one that is going to be destroyed.

My hand pauses on the door of the library. I really hope he smiles at me again. His smiles are wonderful. They make it seem like everything is all right with the world.

I open the door with far more trepidation than is necessary. He hasn't noticed me, his attention fixed on the computer screen. He is tapping his nose with his finger in the endearing way he does when he thinks. The burnished auburn in his hair is clear in this light. How did I ever think he was plain? Was there something wrong with my eyes? He is breathtakingly stunning.

He looks up, and my heart skips a beat, but he doesn't smile. He frowns and looks back at the screen.

"I'm not ripe," he snaps.

It feels like I have been punched in the gut. Hard. I can feel all my tentative hope shattering. This little ember of promise that Colby gave me with his dazzling smiles and his soft noises in bed, is winking out and there is nothing I can do. It's like trying to hold water in my hand.

"I know," I say reflexively and it sounds cold and harsh to my own ears. I should have asked what was wrong or why he is upset, but part of me doesn't want to hear about my own failings.

He looks up at me again and bites down on his bottom lip as if he is trying not to speak. A long, silent moment passes. Then he lets out a big breath.

"How could you let your little brother think his assault was his fault!" he demands angrily, his eyes flashing.

What? I was not expecting this. Has he been talking to Jem? Or the staff? What is going on? What assault? I have no idea what to say. I'm suddenly in a stormy sea, adrift and with no compass.

"Mr. Richards rapes your brother and you deal with it by victim blaming!"

I'm blinking blankly but I can't stop it. His words are not making any sense. I feel as if I am floundering.

"He wasn't raped, and I dealt with it just fine!" I protest as some part of my mind finds the words.

I'd been twenty-six at the time and our parents had just died. All things considered, I did a grand job at hushing everything up and saving the family name. And the very idea of Colby's accusation is making me shake. If anyone ever hurt Jem, I'd destroy them. But that's not what happened. Where is he getting these ideas from?

Colby jumps to his feet, his chair tipping back behind him. His face is flushed with anger.

"Do you even know what consent is?" he yells.

It feels like one of those trick questions, where there is no right answer. I think I know the dictionary definition of that word but I have a sinking feeling Colby means something else.

I have a ridiculous urge to get my phone out and Google it, but I resist and stare back at Colby as if I'm calm and unruffled.

He glares at me for a moment longer, before throwing his hands up in disgust and storming out. Hopelessly, I watch him leave. I feel cold and the darkness is more consuming than ever. He already hates me. I've ruined everything.

I take a deep breath. Fuck it. This is a good thing. I don't understand how or why, but he has finally seen me for who I really am. I have no idea what he is furious about, but it's perfectly clear that there is not going to be any more sweetness or kindness from him. Which means I don't need to try to be nice. My stupid little daydream of him somehow saving me is crushed.

This is a good thing. I can be my true self.

Chapter Twelve

Colby

Eating dinner alone in my rooms is rather depressing, and it's hard not to feel homesick. My parents and I always ate together, usually along with two or three guests. There were always people staying over. A revolving door of company and interesting conversation.

The urge to call my parents is strong, but it will only make me feel worse when I hang up. It would be a temporary reprieve at best and a stark reminder of all that I have lost at worst.

Sighing forlornly, I move the broccoli around my plate. I should not have talked to Harry like that. It's not the done thing. Vessels are supposed to be respectful at all times. I'm terrible at this. Why did I ever think I'd be good at it?

I wonder if I would have ever lost my temper with Rakeswell? But there is no point in going down that train of thought. I'll never know. It's not like I have a crystal ball. Rakeswell is probably riddled with secrets too. Most powerful men are.

It's a morose thought. And it's all very unfair. All I want is a husband and a pleasant life. Someone amenable. I'm not foolish enough to dream of fireworks and soul searing love, but someone to rail me occasionally, and then have breakfast with, is not a lot to ask for. It shouldn't feel so out of reach.

It's not, I tell myself firmly. I just need to make amends with Harry. This is all just a slight hiccup, I'm sure. Harry will forgive me and everything will be fine. He seems happy enough to rail me so I already have one part of my goal achieved. I just need to get him to like me a little more, so that he wants to spend breakfast with me. It's not an insurmountable task.

The door opens and Harry walks in as if I conjured him with my thoughts. I scramble to wipe my mouth with the serviette and to stand at the same time.

"Good evening," I say.

Maybe I should add a formal address? A 'My Lord Husband' or 'Husband'? But being formal can be so cold and I want to bring us closer together, not drive us further apart.

"Good evening, Consort," he replies stonily and there is a coldness in his eyes that wasn't there before.

My heart sinks. I have really, truly, spectacularly messed up. This is going to take a lot of fixing. I sure hope I am up to the task.

"I am hosting a party tomorrow evening," Harry says.

I stare at him completely dumbfounded as my mind tries to make sense of his words. I have a horrifying feeling that I know exactly what he means but my mind is refusing to accept it.

"A party, party?" I ask slowly. "Not a dinner party, or a recital, or a soiree, or a garden party?" The hopeful tone in my voice is cringeworthy.

He flashes me a truly wicked grin. "No, an orgy," he confirms, and my world comes crashing down.

I can only stare. I've never been to one, of course. They are not a place for virgin vessels to be. But I know they are fairly common in certain circles. I should have guessed that Duke Sothbridge was in one of those circles. It fits his reputation perfectly.

"You will attend," he says.

My mouth is dry and my heart is thrumming so loudly I cannot hear anything else. He is my master, my mage. He has the right to order that I go, and there is not a thing I can do about it. In the more traditional circles of society, as is still written into our laws, consent is a privilege that vessels are not accorded. I should not have been surprised about Jem's past. I stupidly forgot just how very progressive my parents and their close friends are. Most people do not think the same.

And It's very clear that Harry does not share my parents' views. I knew he was more traditional, but this traditional? I should have done more research on him. But what would that have achieved? After my little stunt, I had to marry him. There was no other option.

But surely, he is not going to make me do this? I just need to talk to him, I need to explain, argue my case. Say something. Anything.

"I... I..." I stammer weakly, hopelessly.

Harry's eyes darken. "You belong to me Colby. I own you. Your body is mine, to do with as I please and it pleases me to give it to others."

His words send shivers down my spine. I'm going to faint. For real this time. Desperately I hold on to the edge of the table and I swear it is the only thing that is keeping me upright. There is going to be no dissuading him. He is resolute. I can not talk my way out of this.

I've been such a naïve, trusting idiot. Hoping for the best, whilst blithely ignoring the dark side of being a vessel until it slaps me in the face. But what could I have done? There was no way I could have avoided this. I was born a vessel and from that moment in the maze, my fate was sealed.

There is no point in whining that Rakeswell would not have done this to me. I don't know for sure. Suddenly, all my cousin Eban's warnings about getting married and that it is not something to look forward to, are crashing around me. But I had no choice. My family was on the brink of ruin. There was no choice. All paths led to this moment.

"Wear a formal receiving gown," Harry snaps.

And with that, he is gone. I blink blankly at the now empty spot where he was standing and somehow I manage to slide back into my chair. I feel as boneless as a noodle. And now cold, harsh reality is starting to sink in.

Oh my god. I'm going to an orgy.

Chapter Thirteen

I've never worn a formal receiving gown before. Never thought I would have to. Calling them old-fashioned is like calling suits of armor last season.

I had one made as part of the wedding preparations because it is traditional. But I thought it would hang in my dressing room, forever. One of those things you have to have but never use. Like the best china.

It does look good though. It's a fancier version of the gown I wore on my wedding night. The silky white material hangs to my ankles and the way it is cut around my hips makes me look very slender. The panel over my chest and stomach, makes everything there look perfectly flat and toned. The sleeves are all billowy and graceful. I look like a cute femboy cosplaying as a Chinese Wuxia Boy Love character.

Just typical. The first and only time in my life that I don't want to look hot and I look the hottest I have ever looked. Why is life so unfair?

Despondently, I give a little turn as I watch myself in the mirror and the gown swishes softly around me. I grimace. The defining feature of a formal receiving gown is the slit at the back.

Right from my ankles all the way up to the small of my back, ending a mere hairsbreadth above my butt crack. The result is that if I stand with perfect posture, the flowing material meets at the back, keeping me covered. But, if I bend over, even just slightly, the two panels separate, swish apart and leave my ass completely exposed.

Ready to receive my husband. Or whoever he chooses to give me to. The shudder that crashes through me is strong enough to rattle my teeth. Maybe I should put on boxer briefs in rebellion. Harry never said anything about what to wear underneath the receiving gown he ordered me to wear.

But, no. Antagonizing him is a terrible idea. I need to win him over, not push him away. And that is not me being soft. Harry has the power to make my life a living hell. This is just the tip of the iceberg of what he can do to me. The only power I have, the only tool at my disposal is my ability to charm him enough that I unleash his good side.

If he has a good side. And if I have the skill to reach it. I shudder again. I know Harry has a good side. I have seen it in his eyes. I felt it in his essence when every part of us entwined during sex.

Thinking of sex, makes me think about the orgy going on downstairs. I had been doing a very good job in pretending it wasn't happening and that I could hide up here forever.

I swallow dryly. I love sex. I spent the last five years of my life whining that I wasn't able to have any. Tonight I get to have all the sex I want. It's going to be amazing.

Harry strides into my dressing room, startling me out of my thoughts. Our eyes meet briefly in the mirror before his gaze leaves to rove all over my body. His eyes darken and I want to preen. He likes what he sees. Maybe he will take me to bed and keep me to himself.

"You are late," he says instead.

"Sorry," I mumble as I try not to feel too crushed. "I'm ready now," I add with a bright smile.

Something like a wince crosses over Harry's ridiculously handsome face but it passes in a flash and he takes my arm and starts leading me down to the party. My feet obey him while my heart stutters and my head spins.

The walk passes in a daze and far too soon, Harry is opening the door to one of the reception rooms and pushing me inside. The party is in full swing and I don't know where to look or how to stop all the noises reaching my ears. Harry abandons me in the middle of the room, walking away to leave me surrounded by a sea of writhing bodies.

I turn around to look pleadingly at him but Harry is already busy caressing the neck of a beautiful young man. My chest tightens and I snatch my gaze away. I don't need to see that. It's stupid to be jealous, but I can't help it. The sight is awful for other reasons too. My last lingering thread of hope was that Harry would want to play with me and I could fulfill my obligations that way.

"Your Grace," a low voice rumbles behind me.

That's me now, I realize with a jolt. I am a duke consort. Just typical that the very first time I am addressed as such, is at a fucking orgy. I whirl to face the speaker, realizing far too late that such a sudden move in a receiving gown, is a sure way to flash the entire room. Oh well, I'm pretty sure everyone is pretty distracted right now.

My eyes widen as I take in who is talking to me. It's Hyde. My cousin Eban's husband. I mean ex-husband.

"My Lord," I manage without stammering.

Hyde's gaze is lingering over every inch of me. I shiver over the force of his scrutiny. He has always looked at me appreciatively. Perhaps a little lecherously. Why oh why did I ever think it was a good idea to flirt with him a little? Was I ever so naïve as to think it was just harmless fun?

He takes my arm and starts leading me over to the corner of the room, as I lament all my life choices. He leads me to a rutting stool. It's not as fancy as the unused one in my bedchamber, but it looks perfectly functional. I swallow.

Hyde gestures at me to bend over it.

This has to be a bad dream, any moment now I'm going to wake up all sweaty and breathless and alone in my bed.

Numbly, I obey and get into position. The cloth of my gown swishes apart, exposing me to Hyde. I fumble for my brace and place it in between my teeth. Finally, I understand its purpose. I don't want to give Hyde any more than I have to. If I stay quiet, there is a part of me that he cannot take.

Tears are flowing down my cheeks. I ignore them. If I move my hand to brush them away, Hyde will know. I feel him step up behind me, and I shudder. I stare out blankly into the room. Misery is clutching at my gut. This is without doubt, the most awful moment of my entire life. I never knew it was possible to feel so hopeless, so scared. I don't want to give my body to anyone else. I want to belong to my husband.

Two bright spots of aquamarine swim in my blurry sight. I'm silently crying too much to see anything, but is that Harry looking at me?

Suddenly he is here, pushing Hyde away by the sound of it.

"Did you hurt him?" Harry snarls at Hyde.

"I haven't touched him yet!" Hyde growls back.

"And you are not going too!" snaps Harry as he grabs my arm.

I stumble and trip after him as he pulls me off of the rutting stool, and out of the orgy and all the way back to my room. He slams the door shut behind us and releases me.

"What is wrong with you!" he demands.

I furiously scrub the tears off of my face. "I'm sorry, let me just clean myself up and I'll come back and entertain your guests."

Harry stares at me with an unreadable expression on his face. He remains motionless. I scurry to the sink and quickly wash my face, then I walk back to him with a smile.

"Okay, I'm ready, let's go back."

I head towards the door but he steps in front of it, blocking it with his body.

"No, you are not going back in there."

I stare up into his aquamarine eyes, "Really?" I breathe hopefully.

He nods, and I burst into tears again, smooshing myself against his chest and curling my fingers into his shirt. His warm arms wrap around me, holding me close and I sob even harder.

"Why... why are you so upset?" he asks softly.

"Only want you," I hiccup.

His hands move to my shoulders and he pushes me away, but it's only to look into my eyes with deep bewilderment.

"Why? You barely know me, and a cock is a cock."

Is that really what he thinks? How is he so damn cold? What the hell is wrong with him?

"I'm sure you love bending over and taking it from everyone and anyone!" I hear myself snap.

His eyes widen and suddenly he is flipping us over so that I am the one pressed against the door. My head thuds against the wood.

"What have you heard! Who have you been talking to!" His eyes are blazing with fury.

My mouth falls open and every word I have ever learned melts away. I have never seen anyone look so enraged, but as I stare helplessly, Harry's expression shifts to one of horror.

"Oh gosh!" he exclaims. "Colby, are you alright? Did I hurt you?"

He moves my head and rubs the back of it. I seem to have lost the power of thought as well as the power of speech. Just like Harry has lost his frigging mind. I have no idea what is happening. I never suspected that he had this side to him. I thought he was calm and collected in his assholeness, but what else is he capable of?

Harry is staring at me in alarm. "Colby, please don't look at me like that!"

"Like... like what?" I stammer breathlessly.

"Like I'm someone to be feared."

Suddenly he drops to his knees and wraps his arms around my legs.

"I'm sorry. Please forgive me. I can't bear to see that look in your eyes," Harry pleads.

I blink slowly, as if I think that will restore reality. Is Harry drunk? High on some tea he took for the party? I don't understand what is going on, but I can feel him trembling. He is at my feet shaking with emotion.

I reach out and run my hand through his hair. His trembling eases a little. Perhaps I'm a softy but I can't bear to see anyone or anything suffer. I should hate this man for the power he has over me and the things he has done. I didn't even like him in the first place, when he was just someone in my wider social circle. But for some reason I can't, and maybe that makes me a foolish optimist, but I can't change who I am.

Without warning, he jumps to his feet and scoops me up in his arms. I manage to bite back my squeal of surprise. He carries me over to the bed and I wonder if he is going to ravish me, but he just arranges me as the little spoon and curls up behind me. I'm a little disappointed at the lack of ravishing, but this is nice.

"I don't deserve you," he says softly.

I've heard that phrase a thousand times before, between friends, in jest. A flippant almost meaningless phrase. I've never heard it spoken with such soul deep conviction. It makes every hair on my body stand up on end. I don't know how to reply to that. I don't even know where to start. So I say nothing and just wriggle closer to him and place my arm over his, where it lies against my stomach.

He gives a sigh that sort of sounds like contentment.

I think we are going to spend the night like this. The evening started with an orgy. Followed by me freaking out and then him freaking out and then we end the night by spooning. Makes perfect sense.

My mind whirls as it tries to make sense of it all. But through all the confusion, one thing shines clearly.

I think my husband is a little broken.

Chapter Fourteen

Something wakes me from my sleep. It's the dark small hours just before dawn and all is quiet and still. Harry is still behind me, in my bed and the flash of sheer joy that gives me is startling. He stayed. He didn't go back to the party. He didn't retreat to his own room. Harry stayed in my bed, with me. This is wonderful. There is hope for our marriage.

And it's just plain nice. I've never slept in the same bed as someone else before. It's so soothing, so intimate. I could get used to this. Snuggling up to him every night and using him as a giant hot water bottle would be bliss.

It's not such a crazy idea as all that. It could happen. It feels like we are so much closer now. Who knew that mutual freak outs could be such a bonding experience. If just one night can change so much, what is a hundred going to do? Time is one thing we have on our side. We are bound together for the rest of our lives. There is going to be time to figure things out.

Time for me to discover who broke my husband. Time for me to help fix him. I might never see another crack in his armor. But I know now. I know that all is not well and that I am going to try my best to do something about it.

A strange noise echoes around the room. Oh, is that what woke me? The sound is laced with so much pain and fear that my heart aches. I roll over to face Harry. Surely he is not the one making that soft, vulnerable noise? It doesn't seem possible that he would be capable of such a thing. Another chink in his armor, a glimpse of the man beneath the illusion of himself that he has created.

I can barely believe I am seeing more of him, so soon after his first little meltdown.

But here is the evidence before me. Even in the dark, I can see that his face is pale and contorted with terror. His body moves weakly, as if he is trying to fight off whatever dark thing is hounding his dreams. He whimpers again and I can't bear it. Did his earlier outburst break a damn within him that was keeping all the dark things at bay? Have his demons been unleashed?

"Harry, wake up," I say as I shake his shoulder.

My touch seems to jolt him like a lightning strike. He jerks up to a sitting position and suddenly I'm sprawling backwards. The entire right side of my face is on fire. I'm seeing stars and I can't breathe.

Harry clicks his fingers and the lights flicker on. Suddenly he is looming over me with a look of absolute horror on his face.

"Gods, Colby! Did I hit you?"

Tentatively I move my jaw, jagged sparks of pain shoot up my face but it all seems to be working.

"Yeah, I think you did," I answer dazedly and I'm surprised I can talk at all.

All those cartoons where they lay there after being knocked down, while birds tweet and fly in a circle above them, now make perfect sense. It's exactly how I feel. In fact, if I squint, I think I can see the little birds.

"Oh my god!" breathes Harry as he buries his face in his hands.

As soon as I can talk again. I'm going to tell him that it is okay. He was having a nightmare, it was an accident. I've been punched in the face before, by a delirious patient, this is a very similar situation and no big deal. I'm not as delicate as all that.

He peers down at me again and the sheer anguish in his stunning eyes takes my breath away. His gentle fingers take my chin and he carefully moves my face, examining me intently.

"Do you need the healer?" he asks.

His words hurt more than his punch. A stark reminder that I am no longer a healer. But I haven't forgotten everything and I'm not bleeding to death. I'm perfectly capable of taking care of this injury myself.

I don't say any of that. Instead, I just shake my head. Harry's eyes fill with even more pain. He can tell I am upset. I should tell him it's the healer thing, not the punch thing that has got me all emotional. I try to gather the words.

Suddenly he throws himself off of the bed and an anguished sob echoes around the room. He flees and the door slams shut behind him. The room feels colder without him. Somehow dimmer, as if he took the light with him.

My chest tightens. I yearn to go after him, to explain, to reassure and comfort. But Harry is a duke. And a powerful mage. Men like that, are brought up to never cry and to certainly never let anyone see them if they do. Not even their husbands.

He won't want me to see his tears. It would savage his pride. As it is, I'm going to have to pretend that I didn't hear his sob as he left. I can't go to him now, I'll only succeed in making him feel embarrassed and humiliated.

Poor Harry. And poor me. What a mess.

Tomorrow, when he has had a chance to resume his composure, replace that emotionless mask that we all wear, I will talk to him. I will tell him that I understand it was an accident. He was asleep and lost in a dark dream. I'm not upset about it. I got a bit emotional over not being a healer anymore. But it's all good. Everything is fine. This incident is not the end of the world.

Gingerly I sit up. I don't think I have concussion. Carefully I pad over to the mirror. It doesn't look too bad. No broken skin, but my eye is already swelling. It's going to look impressive in the morning. And it is starting to throb now.

Sighing, I pull the bell. I need some ice and a poultice.

What a night.

Chapter Fifteen

My plan to corner Jem at lunch and ask discreet questions about Harry, is not going very well. I'm starving, and peeking into the lunchroom and seeing the luncheon meats, cucumber sandwiches and the fillet of salmon is torture. This is going to be the last time I'm going to be able to walk away. If he is not there next time I check, then sod it.

My stomach rumbles in agreement. My attempt to get to the bottom of Harry's secrets is going to have to wait for another day. And that's fine. None of this is going to be a quick fix. Discovering why Harry is so haunted and troubled is not going to give the key to fixing him. It's merely going to be the first step. Once I understand why, I can figure out a way to help him.

Despite my good intentions, I can't help feeling guilty for my nosey plan. It is an invasion of privacy, but then again, how can I help if I don't know what is going on?

A heavy sigh escapes me. Maybe I should mind my own business and trust that Harry will tell me, if he wants me to know. But then men like Harry have been raised to take their troubles and secrets to the grave. I'm doing the right thing, I know I am.

I just need to wait a little longer, and then I can check the lunch room again. The staff will be clearing everything away soon. Jem is bound to make an appearance before too long. I'm sure the man eats.

I pace my sitting room for five whole minutes before dashing back to the lunchroom. As I peek through the door hinges, I see Jem heaping salmon on his plate. I have never seen a more wonderful sight. He is here! I can talk to him and I can finally eat.

"Good afternoon!" I call cheerily as I stroll in.

Jem looks up at me and nods in greeting. His gaze flicks to my bruised face. He doesn't look shocked or surprised, and somehow I just know it isn't because his brother is a brute. It's because Harry told him. A spark of happiness ignites within me. Harry has someone to talk to. I wish it was me, but I'm glad he is not all alone in the world. One day I will earn his trust, but in the meantime he has Jem, and that makes me happy.

I grab a plate and start loading it with all the delicious-looking food. My mouth is watering. I hope my stomach doesn't give an embarrassingly loud rumble.

"Lovely weather!" I gush, for something to say.

Jem glances at the window and the rain lashing it and the gray sky beyond. He raises an eyebrow. "For ducks."

Oh damn it, what is wrong with me? How can I be messing this up already! Okay, I need to rally.

"Absolutely! Why should sunny days get all the love?"

Jem stares at me as if he thinks I have lost my mind, but then a wry smile stretches across his face and he shakes his head in a gesture that looks almost fond. It warms my heart and makes me feel a little gooey inside. It's better than I deserve, considering how intense and personal our last conversation was.

"I'm sorry if I crossed the line," I blurt.

Crossed the line? I pole vaulted over it and then obliterated it with dynamite. And that's putting it mildly. Jem has every right to never talk to me again. But he smiles softly again and clearly catches on to what I am rambling about.

"You have nothing to apologize for."

I smile at him, and we take our plates over to the table and sit down.

"Did Harry have a happy childhood?" I say whilst trying to appear all sweet and innocent.

I'm met with a stony glare. Then Jem's eyes linger on my swollen eye, and he relents with a soft sigh.

"When he was fourteen, he outgrew our father in terms of spell casting ability, so he was sent to apprentice with Earl Rathbone for two years. The whole thing was terribly hush, hush because we couldn't let anyone know that father was less than competent."

Jem winces, as if he feels bad for even saying that much about his deceased father. But he takes a breath and continues.

"Rathbone's oldest was nineteen, away at university, but it meant Rathbone had recent experience of teenage boys and teaching them magic. It seemed like an excellent arrangement."

Jem pauses again.

"I was only four, but even I could see that Harry was never the same again. It was like the light went out of him."

A silence falls. I cannot think of a single thing to say to that. It's awful. It's tragic. I wish it had never happened. But it has and all I can do is try to help Harry deal with the consequences.

My gaze meets Jem's and the hope I see in them is daunting. He wants me to help his brother. He thinks I might be able to do it. I have no idea why he thinks so highly of me and I very much doubt I can live up to it. But I'm going to try my best.

He reads my intention and gives a satisfied nod. We resume eating in silence while my thoughts whirl. What a tragic family I have married into. First whatever happened to Harry while he was in Rathbone's care, then their parents dying, followed by Jem being assaulted and subsequently being ruined in the eyes of society.

My entrapment of Harry must have made them feel like they were under a family curse or something. Familiar feelings of guilt start to twist through me and I try to quash them down. It was an accident, I meant them no ill will and now I am here, I'm going to do everything I can to be a blessing to this family. For better or worse, it's my family now.

Chapter Sixteen

The television talks to itself while I vaguely stare at it. My face is gently throbbing and my mind is whirling with a thousand thoughts. Cornering Jem at lunch has given me plenty to think about.

I'm sitting here as I try to recall everything I know about Earl Rathbone. Considering he has been a recluse for a decade, buried in his alchemy work, there has been a lot of gossip about him recently. The first thing that comes to mind is that Earl Hathbury challenged him to a duel for his vessel and won. Then Rathbone's son, Lord Garrington, declared his love for his own brother, who turned out not to be his brother at all because Rathbone had been cuckolded by his second wife, but the earl still disowned his son for it.

I frown. Wait a minute. It might have been the other way around, disowning the son first and then losing his vessel to Hathbury. Either way, that's a lot of scandal in just a couple of years.

I sit up straighter as a puzzle piece falls into place. It was Lord Garrington's not-brother that Harry assaulted on a balcony and tried to claim as his vessel. The event which led to him fighting a duel with Lord Garrington. Harry lost, but then Garrington ended up being disowned a few months later, so that must have eased the sting a little.

But what if there was more to the story than that? What if it was more than Harry not being able to keep his hands to himself while coveting a beautiful and powerful vessel? It is a striking coincidence that it was the supposed son of the man he was secretly apprenticed to.

Had it been revenge?

Had the plan been to obtain Fennrick Montfort as his vessel? But then what? Surely Harry would not make an innocent man pay for the crimes of his father? I don't think Harry is so malicious. Maybe the plan was just to piss Rathbone off by claiming his son? Who turned out not to be his son. Did Harry know that part? Gah! This is so confusing.

I sigh and rub my forehead. Mysteries within mysteries. I have a feeling there is going to be a huge tangled web of them to sort through. It's a little daunting. Will I ever be able to get to the bottom of it all? Do I even need to? Perhaps I'm going down the wrong path. I can be supportive without knowing the ins and outs of everything. Prodding around might let the cat out of the bag or open a can of worms or whatever similar saying is appropriate.

My thoughts are scattered by Harrison, the butler, knocking sharply on my door and entering. He looks as formidable as ever, with a flawless posture that I can only dream of.

"Earl and Countess Devonshire are seated in the drawing room, your Grace."

"My parents?" I gasp as I jump to my feet.

"Yes," Harrison replies drolly as if he thinks I am completely daft for thinking there may be a different Earl and Countess Devonshire.

I dash down to the drawing room in a giddying wave of excitement and as I approach the door, I hear my mother's voice telling Father her opinion on the fireplace. I feel a grin stretch across my face. It is so lovely that they are here.

"Why didn't you tell me you were coming!" I admonish gently as I open the door.

"Well maybe if you answered our calls, we might have been able to! You do know how to worry a mother, darling," she says as she turns around.

Her bright smile fades as she sees me. The color drains from her face. Concerned, I glance at father but he is similarly aghast. What is wrong?

Oh gosh, I completely forgot about my black eye! What on earth am I going to say? Harry's night terrors and his vulnerabilities are far too intimate to share. They are not my secrets to give. I'm going to have to think of something.

"I... um... walked into a door," I say lamely.

I'm not sure I would believe me, and I certainly haven't convinced my parents, judging by their expressions. Just fabulous. Now my parents think that Harry is beating me. They are going to try to take me home with them and I've unleashed a whole new drama into my life that I am going to have to deal with.

What else is going to go wrong?

"Come sit down and let me pour the tea!" exclaims Mother.

Sheepishly, I obey her and let them both fuss over me for a minute. It does feel lovely and I do love attention.

"We miss you, Son. Why don't you come home with us for the weekend?" says Father.

I put down my cup of tea and look them both steadily in the eye.

"I'm fine. It was a genuine accident."

They exchange glances before turning back to me. They look slightly mollified but not entirely convinced.

"My cycle hasn't settled yet, so I can't go far, anyway." I add.

The crestfallen look on my father's face is too much to bear, so I look away.

"If there was anything we could help with, you would tell us? Wouldn't you, my dear?" asks my mother softly.

"Of course!" I answer with a bright smile. "Now tell me how everything is at home, have you been able to fix the roof?"

My aim at distraction is probably terrible and blatant, but it is worth a try. I look at them hopefully and then realize with a sinking heart that it was absolutely the wrong thing to say. Both their faces fall and they look devastated. I can just tell they are thinking that they sold their youngest son to an abusive husband so that they could clear their debts and fix the leaking roof.

It's not what I meant at all. Now what do I do?

"Oh, I made a new friend! Harry's brother, Jem. He is lovely!"

Mother's brow scrunches in confusion. "Sothbridge has a brother?"

Now would be a perfect time for the ground to open up and swallow me whole. Or just give me a spade so I can dig this hole for myself faster. What a disaster! My parents do not need to know that I am living with a disgraced vessel and I have absolutely no right to share Jem's past with them, especially just to make them feel better about the situation.

"Er... yes... he is a vessel and doesn't partake in society." As backpedals go, it has to be one of the worst ones ever. Nobody chooses to not partake in society.

Mother's nostrils flare like a bloodhound catching a scent. "Tell me everything."

My heart sinks and I take a cup of tea to buy some precious time. How on earth am I going to get out of this one?

Chapter Seventeen

I roll over in bed again. I can't sleep. I can't even get comfortable. I should be exhausted after dealing with my parents all afternoon. It's a miracle I ever got them to leave, though I am now bound in a promise to call them every day. It's going to make me homesick, and it's going to be awful lying to them every day, but it's worth it if it stops them from fretting. And I won't be completely lying, it's not like my marriage is the worst marriage of all time. There is just some choppy waters to navigate.

Ugh! Now I am too hot. A minute ago I was too cold. Kicking the covers off as if they are personally responsible for everything, doesn't make me feel any better. Is there anything that will?

A wave of dizziness washes over me and with it comes realization. I am ripe. So very full of magic that I have no idea how I missed it.

I bite my bottom lip in uncertainty. It's the middle of the night. Do I go to Harry now, or try to ride it out until morning? The proper thing is to go to him. I know that much. But the thought of waking him up feels uncomfortable. Will he have to throw on a robe to answer the door, because he sleeps naked?

Will his golden hair be all sleep tousled? Will he be happy to see me?

Thinking of Harry fills my mind full of all sorts of erotic images. Very enticing and extremely alluring ones. Did I always think he was irresistibly sexy, or is it my magic being obsessed? I guess I will never know. All I know is that the thought of being in his arms has me throwing off my covers and jumping out of bed. I want his hands on me. I want the feel of his soft lips. I'm ripe, he won't deny me. My magic will be calling to him like a siren's song.

But I can't run to him. I should at least shower first. And then I need to put a gown on, just a simple white one like I wore on my wedding night. I also need my brace. It feels like a lot to remember but I know there is even more. I think I'm supposed to knock on his door and kneel. There are some formal words to say too, but I can't for the life of me remember what they are. My crash course in vessel etiquette was a poor substitute for two years of training and it's hard not to feel inadequate. Even though I'm fairly certain Harry doesn't care.

I have the quickest, yet still thorough, shower, in the history of showers. Then I get stuck putting the stupid gown on because I was in too much of a hurry to dry myself properly and the cloth is sticking to my damp skin. After some swearing and struggling, I get untangled and get the blasted thing on. I grab my brace and head for Harry's room.

As I knock on his door a wave of adrenaline rushes through me, leaving me trembling softly. Most of it is excited anticipation, but I am also concerned if Harry is going to be happy to see me. The allure of my magic will be enticing but I want him to feel more than dutiful. I want him to want me, not just my magic.

The door opens, and the sight of him takes my breath away. His hair is shining and his eyes sparkling. He is dressed in soft gray pajamas and fully awake. He was expecting me. He steps aside to let me in but I'm transfixed by his perfect chest and well-defined arms. He even smells amazing, all masculine and musky. I could breathe it in forever.

He gently takes my hand and coaxes me to step forward, into his room. I've never been in here before. It's nice. And covered in musical instruments and sheet music. Harry is a musician? I had no idea. I turn to him in confusion, but the gentle smirk on his face and the dark gleam in his eyes, tells me that music is the last thing on his mind right now. He is definitely happy to see me and the knowledge sends a warm tingle down my spine.

I am caught helplessly in his intense gaze. The way he is looking at me stirs a heat deep in my belly. My mouth goes dry and I can't swallow.

Suddenly I'm lying on a soft mattress and Harry is above me. We are on the bed now? How did that happen? He leans down and I manage to suck in a breath just before his lips brush my own, feather soft. He is heat and passion. Lust and need. The taste of him ignites my soul. My arms encircle his neck and hungry moans flow out of me. His tongue flicks into my mouth and my back arches, seeking more of him. Reaching for him. I need every inch of him pressing against every inch of me.

His hands slip under my gown and explore my body, his touch leaving a trail of fire etched into my skin. He makes every cell in my body sing with joy. His fingers find my hole and tease me with a soft caress. Damn it, I forgot to lube up again.

Harry breaks from our kiss and looks down at me. His lips are swollen and his eyes dark. He looks more handsome than ever.

"Turn over for me," he asks.

Wordlessly I obey. His firm hands pull my ass cheeks apart and then his hot tongue lathes my hole, sending shockwaves of pleasure shooting everywhere. The noise that comes out of me is ungodly and Harry pauses in his administrations to chuckle his appreciation. Thankfully, he soon resumes.

His tongue tortures and torments me. Driving me to levels of ecstasy I never knew existed. I'm clutching the sheets as if they can save me. As if holding onto them is going to stop me from being catapulted into another realm of existence. It's not working. I am in a whole new reality. One where my body writhes and undulates with pleasure and the only thing that exists is lust and Harry. Our very own realm, where we are the only beings. Where I am breathing light and exuding magic.

Everything is swirling and building in a crescendo within me. Gathering like a storm. Any moment now, it's going to unleash like a supernova.

Harry's tongue is gone, and his cock is pushing at my entrance. Whimpering I lift my ass up towards him, welcoming the intrusion, craving it, needing it. I want to be impaled. Filled. Stretched. I want to feel Harry's heat inside me. I want to be made complete. I need him to thrust the emptiness away. *Take me. Own me. I am yours.*

He eases inside me and it is everything I was yearning for and far, far more. I'm screaming in pleasure and satisfaction and

I can't stop. His strong hands claim my hips and he thrusts. Pushing me into the mattress and driving me to even more insane levels of bliss.

The rhythm he picks up is brutal and wonderful. My whole body rocks to it while I sob with ecstasy. I don't want this perfect moment to ever, ever stop. I want him to rail me forever, keep me lost in this mindless pleasure. Nothing has ever felt so good.

But my orgasm is close, so very close. When it comes, my magic will explode out of me and I will be spent. Futility I try to keep it at bay. Try to resist, to prolong my euphoria. But it's like trying to hold back the tide. Harry shifts his angle, and it's one shot of sensation too much. My orgasm detonates. Sweeping away everything in its path.

Including my consciousness.

Chapter Eighteen

Drifting awake feels like floating in a warm current. Awareness slowly coalesces around me. There are soft, clean sheets against the bare skin of my back. Plump pillows are cradling my head. Warm covers are tucked up to my chin. I'm naked and clean. And I am alone in my own bed.

Did Harry clean me up, then carry me to my own bed and tuck me up? It's still dark outside so I cannot tell how much time has passed. My chest tightens. He did tenderly care for me, which is much more than most vessels usually get, but he also dumped me back in my room when he was done with me. And I can't help but feel rejected. I'd much prefer to wake up sticky and messy and in his arms.

Sighing forlornly, I roll onto my side and tuck up into a fetal position. It doesn't mean he doesn't care. He is merely behaving properly and doing what he has been taught must be done.

I hug myself tighter. Of course it could absolutely mean that he doesn't care. That I'm nothing but a vessel to him. But why am I expecting anything else? We were practically strangers not long ago, and he wasn't exactly pleased about having to marry me. He is hardly going to fall madly in love in just a few weeks. These things take time. Nevermind the dark secrets he is hiding.

At least the sex is good.

A very undignified snort laugh escapes me and I'm so glad there is no one here to hear that. Oh dear, now I can feel myself about to descend into hysterical giggling. I'm losing my mind.

I'm clearly not going to go back to sleep and I don't want to lie here either moping or laughing maniacally. That means only one thing. Hot chocolate.

Throwing on some pajamas and a plush dressing gown, I'm soon padding down the dimly lit and still hallways. It's a little creepy, but I'm used to large, old houses. There is no need to be a baby about it.

The lights are on in the kitchen, and it is warm in here. I can't help my little sigh of relief. Suddenly someone walks out of the larder at the back of the room and I nearly scream in fright. But it's just Jem. He is wearing teal silk pajamas and has no right looking so glamorous in the middle of the night.

"Are you alright?" he asks with concern in his eyes.

I feel myself flush. He is not asking about the fright he just gave me or the fact I'm wandering around in the dark of night. He would have been able to sense I was ripe earlier. And now he can tell I'm not ripe. Which means only one thing. I have tumbled with his brother.

"I... I'm fine," I stammer. "Just after hot chocolate."

Jem smiles and holds up the tub of cocoa in his hands. "Great minds think alike. Take a seat, I'll make it."

Smiling in return I sit at the oak table in the center of the room. I nearly whimper as my backside touches the hard wood of the chair, but I manage to hide it just in time. I feel more well used than truly sore, anyway. Maybe I'm a pervert, but I like the feeling so it would be awkward as hell to receive any sympathy for it. Nevermind that it was Jem's brother that did this to me, an image I'm sure he'd rather not think about.

Jem stirs a pot of milk on the range. It's strange to see him acting so domesticated. My first impression of him, painted a picture of a wild, exuberant hellion. But he clearly has far more sides to him than that.

A few minutes later, he sits across from me and slides a mug of delicious looking hot chocolate over the table and into my waiting hands.

"Thank you," I say before taking a sip and sighing with contentment. Just what I needed. There is nothing like a warm cup of coco.

"Harry is my brother and I love him dearly," Jem begins carefully. "But he can be such an asshole sometimes."

I don't know what to say to that. I don't think there is a polite response. Defending Harry implies Jem is lying. Agreeing with Jem, insults my husband.

Jem's aquamarine eyes, so much like his brother's, regard me intently and don't relent in the slightest. "Is he treating you well?"

I hate that I have to think about that question. Things certainly haven't been a fairy tale, but what arranged marriage is? He hasn't beaten me. The cruelest thing he has done was take me to the orgy, but then he changed his mind. The worst thing is the distance he keeps between us. Does all that count as treating me well? I have no idea.

And now I have hesitated far too long, and that's an answer all in itself. Jem's eyes are full of compassion.

"I have every faith things will improve," I hear myself say.

Jem smiles, "So do I. Once he gets to know you and learns he can trust you, everything will be lovely. If not, let me know and I'll slap him for you."

The mental image that paints makes me grin, I can well imagine Jem doing such a thing. I almost want to see it. And that's a truly wicked thought. I need to take a sip of my hot chocolate to hide my giggle.

The warming drink soothes me, and I finally notice Jem's magic. He is going to be ripe soon. Probably tomorrow. That explains why he is up in the middle of the night. Who is going to empty him? I want to ask. But it is none of my business and frightfully personal. I hope he has one person who helps him regularly, but I have a sinking feeling that Jem is given to a different mage every time. All condoned by Harry. Possibly arranged by him.

I drink some more of my hot chocolate but I can't taste it over the sudden bitterness in my mouth. Maybe I'm a foolish, naïve and immature child, refusing to see that my husband is not a good person. Ignoring all the evidence before me.

A weary sigh escapes me. I just don't know. At some point the truth, whatever that may be, will rise up and slap me in the face, and I will just have to deal with it when it does.

Chapter Nineteen

I feel sick and I don't think it's because of David's driving. Harry's driver is extremely professional. I'm pretty sure I'm nauseous because I'm headed to my first formal event as Duke Consort Sothbridge and given the scandalous nature of our engagement and the hasty wedding that followed, all eyes are going to be on us.

I always used to dream of being the center of attention but now it has finally come to pass, I'm discovering that actually I'd rather not be the focal point. Drifting around mostly unseen and unnoticed like I used to, sounds heavenly. I sigh, be careful what you wish for, I guess.

Harry shoots me a concerned look at my sigh, but says nothing. Instead, he turns his attention back to the window. I think our silence is companionable and not hostile. I can't think of anything to say because being in the back of a car with him is very distracting. I'm not ripe. I'm not even anywhere near ripe, yet the desire to crawl onto his lap is strong. If it gets any worse, I'm going to have to cling onto the door handle to stop myself.

In my defense, he looks ridiculously handsome in his perfectly fitting tux. I don't think anybody would be able to resist. The man certainly has a presence. Something more than his magic or the innate confidence that men of his status have been raised to wear. It's something I always noticed about him, even when I didn't like him. A presence that fills the space around him. In the back of a car, it's overwhelming. I feel like I'm drowning in him and it's a great way to go.

The crunch of gravel underneath the tires jolts me from my musings. We have arrived, and it feels far too soon. A swarm of butterflies takes flight in my stomach. I'm here and people are going to be staring at me. I'm so glad I was naughty and used a smidgen of my magic to heal my eye.

Harry jumps out of the car and walks around to open my door for me. It's a lovely gesture. I smile at him as I climb out. He smiles back and takes my arm. Okay, now my butterflies are turning into happy ones. I know it's probably just for show, but I don't care. I'm on Harry's arm and that's all that matters.

The walk into the house and through the hallways to the ballroom, passes in a happy daze and suddenly I'm standing at the top of a small flight of stairs and facing everyone who has already arrived at the ball.

"Duke and Duke Consort Sothbridge," announces the butler loudly.

A million pair of eyes turn to look at us. I hear a few gasps and a multitude of excited whispers. The room is too hot and my clothes are too tight.

"Pay them no heed," says Harry quietly, while still looking dead ahead. "They are as worthless as their opinion of you."

Keeping my eyes forward feels like trying to resist the gravity of a black hole. I really want to look at him. Somehow, I don't and somehow I make it down the stairs without landing on my face. Probably because I am clinging onto his arm so tightly.

As soon as we reach the bottom, Harry is swarmed by people. He is a popular man and no doubt people are also keen to harvest fuel for gossip. I need to plaster a happy, contented smile on my face. But not too contented. I don't want to look smug or like the cat who got the cream. I need to convey that the maze incident was a happy accident. Gods this is hard! I'm sweating so much, it's gross. Thank heavens my suit is dark and no one is actually going to see my sweat stains.

I let the conversation wash over me until Lord Greyfield's words catch my attention.

"May I steal you away to the billiards room, old chap? I have some business matters I'd like to discuss."

Glumly, I release my hold on Harry's arm, but to my surprise, Harry doesn't walk away, he turns to me.

"Will you be alright?"

There is genuine concern in his dazzling eyes. I nod and smile. I can't keep him from important business. Heaven knows I'm doing enough of that already by tethering him to me until my cycle settles.

He nods in return, untangles his arm from my grip and walks away with Greyfield. I'm not going to watch him go. I'm going to accept a flute of champagne from this server and I'm going to watch the dancers like I haven't a care in the world.

The little crowd that had formed around Harry, melts away, leaving me standing alone. It's fine, this is fine. I'll see someone I know well soon enough. I don't think I'm a social pariah. I bloody well hope not, anyway. I guess I will find out by the end of the evening. But at least I was invited, unlike Jem or my parents.

Champagne bubbles burn my nose as I drink it far too quickly. I really hope my parents' lack of invitation is not society believing my entrapment of Harry was all their idea. They only helped me in my plan, they weren't the instigator. The scheme was all mine. Well, trapping Rakeswell was my aim. Catching Harry instead was fate's plan. Or just plain bad luck.

No, it was good luck, I suddenly realize. I like Harry. I'm happy I'm married to him and not Rakeswell.

"Your Grace, would you give me the pleasure of this dance?"

I blink in surprise at Viscount Baxby. The man is older than my father and not known for dancing. Is he mining for gossip? I should decline, but wait a minute. He is a close friend of Earl Rathbone, the man Harry was secretly apprenticed to. I might be able to learn something.

I smile, place my empty glass on the table behind me and let Baxby lead me out to the dancefloor. It's been an age since I danced. My body is thrumming with excitement. I lose myself in the joy of movement for a while.

"Harry has good taste," says Baxby, bringing me back to reality with a bump.

Startled, I glance up at him. The look in his eye reminds me of the way Hyde was looking at me at the orgy. My mouth has gone dry. I try to step away but his grip on me tightens.

"Now, now, don't cause a scene by leaving in the middle of a dance."

He is right. It will cause a scene. Besides, it's just a dance. Baxby isn't going to molest me on the dancefloor. I can cope with another few minutes of this.

His hand slips down from the small of my back. Okay, he can't molest me but I guess he can cop a feel.

Suddenly, I crash into someone. Harry. I would recognize the feel of him anywhere. His strong hand grabs my arm. I look up at him but his aquamarine eyes are fixed on Baxby.

"Hell hath no fury like the fury I will unleash if you touch him," Harry growls.

The hairs on the back of my neck rise. There is something very real in his threat. I just have time to see Baxby turn an unhealthy shade of pale before Harry is dragging me off of the dancefloor. I'm much shorter than him, I haven't got a chance in keeping up with his long, determined stride. But he doesn't let up. As we reach the edge of the dancefloor, he barks at a member of staff.

"Show us to our room!"

The poor man nods and scurries ahead. The hallways pass in a blur of dark wood and plush carpets. Then the staff member opens a door and Harry pulls me into a very nice bedchamber. Complete with a fourposter bed. Just the one. One bed. Harry is going to have to spend the night with me. Unless he decides we are to go home.

The door shuts. We are alone. I can almost taste Harry's anger, the air is so thick with it.

"S...Sorry," I stammer.

He lets go of me and shakes his head. "You did nothing wrong."

Belatedly, I remember to breathe and I suck in a great lung full of air. Harry rubs his hands over his face and then his hair.

"I never should have brought you to this nest of vipers."

Should I disagree with him? Remind him that it's just a ball? The same social circle that I have been mixing in all my life? But I guess I wasn't Duke Consort Sothbridge before. Thinking about it, that changes everything. Harry's enemies are now my own. They may well seek me out as a way to get to Harry. It's like I was a pawn that somehow made it to the far end of the chessboard and suddenly I'm a queen and now everyone is going to try to attack me. But If I have done nothing wrong, then neither has Harry.

However, it's clear he doesn't see it that way. He looks very distraught. It seems that I did learn some things from dancing with Baxby. Harry really doesn't like him. And something bad definitely happened while he was apprenticed. Now I just need to figure out what it was, and then find a way to help Harry heal from it.

"I can just stay here," I offer. "I am feeling quite tired."

It can't be any later than eight in the evening, but nevermind. Harry clearly has business to attend to. I know he doesn't attend these things for fun. If I retire early, he won't have to worry about my safety. Then before our next social event, he is going to have to tell me who his enemies are and let me know how I can defend myself against them. I can't be a supportive husband, if I don't know what the hell is going on.

Harry gives me a conflicted look. I can tell he is tempted by the idea, but feels bad about it. I pull my phone out of my pocket.

"I can entertain myself. I'll get all comfy in that bed and wait for you."

His eyes light up with fiery interest at my cheeky suggestion and it sends a flare of arousal coursing through me. Judging by the way he is looking at me, I'm pretty sure I'm going to get lucky tonight. Which is fantastic. It will be the first time he has touched me when I'm not ripe, and It will be wonderful to be his husband and not just his vessel.

"Are you sure?" he asks.

"Very," I answer, with what I hope is a naughty wink, even though I know he wasn't asking if I was sure about offering bedroom activities.

He gives me a wry smile and I want to drag him over to the bed right now. Cement this new step forward in our relationship, as well as get well and truly railed. But he moves away, to the window and checks that it is locked. Then he comes back to me.

"Lock the door after me and open it for no one," he says.

I nod my understanding.

His warm fingers caress my chin, and then his lips are on mine. I bite back my squeak of surprise. I should give a sexy moan instead but I can only melt before him, the feel of his kiss sends shockwaves through me that turn my bones to jelly. So much so that he has to hold me up.

He breaks the kiss and I can't stop my hungry, needy whimper. He grins and runs a finger, feather soft across my swollen lips.

"Later," he promises. "I won't be long."

He bloody well better not be. Because now I'm very hard and I don't want to sort myself out once he is gone. I want to save all my stamina for him.

He grins at me again. A devilish, sexy smirk that promises depravity. It makes me even harder. But he slips out of the door. I lock it and lean my forehead against the wood as if it somehow makes me closer to him.

I really hope he doesn't keep me waiting for long.

Chapter Twenty

A soft knock on the door jolts me awake. I can't believe I fell asleep. The way I run to the door is utterly shameless and I don't even care.

"Harry?" I remember to check.

"It's me." His deep voice rumbles through the wood and makes me shiver.

I unlock the door and fling it open. His stunning eyes rake all over me before returning to my face and grinning.

"Look at you," he smirks.

Oh gosh, I have bed hair, don't I! Hurriedly I try to smooth my crazy hair down but he just chuckles as he steps into the room and locks the door behind him.

My red satin pajamas are all wrinkled. My eyes are probably all blurry. I'm terrible at being sexy. While he just stands there in his tux looking like sex incarnate and I just know he is not even trying. It's so unfair.

He steps up to me and his fingers tug at my top. My breath hitches and I'm caught helpless in his gaze. Heaven knows why, but judging by the look in his eyes, he likes what he sees. There is no accounting for taste I suppose.

"I think these should come off," he rumbles.

Shakily, my fingers fly up to my buttons and try to obey him. His eyes darken as he watches me intently. As if my fumbling is a sexy strip show. I have no idea what causes it, but I am so very glad he sees me that way. The heat in his gaze ignites a fire deep in my belly, and between us it feels like we are heating up the very air. Turning it into something viscous and sensual. Something that caresses my skin and strokes my arousal.

Finally, I finish with the last button. I shrug the fabric off of my shoulders and let it fall to the floor. He sucks in a breath and that makes me tingle all over. I'm much swifter with the drawstring of the trousers. The satin falls with a swish to pool at my ankles.

Harry's eyes linger on my very hard cock. He hasn't even touched me and I'm already hard for him. He seems to appreciate that. A lot.

"Get on the bed," he orders.

I step out of my pajamas with a modicum of grace and lie on my back on the bed, in what I hope is an inviting sprawl.

Harry groans, and strides over to the bedside cabinet. "For the love of all things holy, there better be lube in here."

He pulls open the draw and then pauses for a moment before chuckling. He picks up a long thin box and holds it up while giving me a wry smile. I know that box. That's the box that holds the magic dildo in it. My mouth falls open in shock.

"I... I let Stephanie pack for me," I protest.

Harry raises an eyebrow and I feel myself flush. Having staff pack for me is very lazy, but she insisted. And by the time I saw this room, the staff here had already unpacked. None of this is my fault.

"Luckily for us, she is excellent at packing," he says as he holds up a giant bottle of lube with his other hand.

My cheeks are on fire now, and I have to look away. I really hope he doesn't think I am so presumptuous. But he seems pleased and not outraged, so I guess it's all good.

"I want you on your hands and knees," says Harry and my stomach flips over and my cock swells even more. Suddenly, I cannot think of anything else.

Wordlessly, I roll over and obey him. My breaths are heavy, as if I have forgotten how to breathe. Harry moves to the foot of the bed. He is staring at my naked ass and nothing has ever felt more intimate.

The lube bottle squelches and then cold gloop hits the top of my butt crack. I yelp in surprise but the sound turns into a moan, as the lube trickles down to my hole. Harry's fingers join it, and he smears the lube around. His touch is like electricity. I cry out and my cock leaks pre-cum.

I want him so much that it hurts. I want the stretch, the burn. The feel of him deep inside of me. Making me his. I crave the pleasure he can give. I desire the intimacy. The feeling of closeness. I want all of him and I want it now.

He eases a finger inside of me and I yowl as my fingers clutch the sheets. The sensation is a taunt and a tease. A mere echo of what I need. I rock my hips back, encouraging him to give me more. He adds a second finger. It's still not enough. He starts a scissoring movement and I moan with joy, more at the knowledge that he is quickly preparing me for the main event, than the sensation itself.

His fingers disappear, and I whimper at the loss but I also shiver in anticipation. But to my surprise, he appears underneath me. Lying on his back and sliding between my legs until his head is level with my cock.

Hot, wet heat envelopes my cock. The sensation curls my toes and throws my head back with a gasp. He is relentless. There is no time to catch my breath as he lavishes my cock with attention. He sucks. He licks. He kisses. Each alternating sensation drives me more and more wild. I'm sobbing and thrusting into his mouth.

Something broad and blunt pushes at my hole. His fingers? No! I howl as I realize what it is. It's the magic dildo. He is going to fuck and suck me at the same time. It's crazy. It's hot. It's going to completely undo me.

He pushes inside me and it feels so much like him, that disorientation makes my head spin. He grunts and sucks me harder. My arms collapse and my face hits the mattress but somehow my knees are still holding up, just enough so that I'm not suffocating him completely.

The dildo slowly stretches and fills me. It's warm and pulsing. Damn, it feels good. There is nothing better than Harry's cock inside me. Either the magic one or the real one.

He starts to move it in and out. A fast rhythm that causes delicious friction. The suction on my cock is intense and his tongue is sliding up and down the underside of my cock in perfect time with his thrusts. It's all too much. My orgasm explodes through me. I can see only stars. Hear only my gasping breaths. Feel nothing but screaming ecstasy.

Slowly my mind comes back online. I'm lying on my back. The dildo is still inside me. Harry is looking down at me. His eyes wide and dark with lust. They flick down to my stuffed and stretched hole.

"You look damn good like that," he growls.

I whimper helplessly.

"I wonder how many times I can make you cum?" he says as his eyes flare.

A strange noise comes out of my throat, and my cock gives a valiant twitch. Harry chuckles. Clearly accepting the invitation. His head lowers. His soft, wet tongue flicks around my rim, where it is stretched around the dildo. The dildo that is also him.

I yell and buck, my eyes rolling to the back of my head. My body is still trembling with aftershocks and everything feels oversensitive. But he shows no mercy and licks me again. I keen, and he chuckles, his breath warm against my most sensitive parts.

It's going to be a long night. A long glorious, wonderful night.

Life has never been better.

Chapter Twenty-One

Harry

Colby yawns sleepily beside me. Without thinking, I reach out and pull him close to me. He looks up at me with a dazzling grin, before settling against my shoulder. The feel of his warm body pressed against mine is intoxicating. We are just sitting in the back of a car, driving through the early morning light towards home. There is no reason for this simple moment to feel so special.

It must just be endorphins from a night of wonderful sex. I'm just thrilled to discover that Colby wants me even when he is not ripe. And he clearly doesn't see it as a martial obligation. He enjoys being with me. Nearly as much as I enjoy him. He is an absolute delight between the sheets. Passionate. Responsive. Honest. Sexier than sin. Being granted the privilege of the pleasure of his body feels like an honor I have not earned.

I'm not going to be able to resist him any longer. Taking him when he is not ripe is going to play havoc with his magic and delay him settling into a rhythm. But I don't think I've ever cared about anything less. I'm already looking forward to tonight.

I need to stop that train of thought before I end up spending the journey home with a boner. Or by ravishing Colby. The latter doesn't even seem like a bad idea at all. Which just goes to show how addled I am.

I need to think about something else. Anything else. An image flashes across my mind, of Baxby with his grubby hands on Colby. I frown. I don't want to think about that, but it is too late. I can already feel an echo of the rage that burned through me at the sight.

How dare Baxby touch what is mine.

Colby is precious and does not deserve to be sullied by the likes of him. I'm going to keep Colby safe, if it is the last thing I do.

A soft snore echoes around the car. Colby is asleep? He feels safe enough with me to not only fall asleep in my presence, but actually leaning on me? How can one person be so utterly adorable?

An uncomfortable feeling settles in my gut. The familiar weight of responsibility. Colby is sweet, naive and innocent. That makes him so very vulnerable. Unable to defend himself. Which means it is all on me. And it feels different than looking after Jem. For one thing my brother is more vicious than an alley cat. For another, this feeling I have for my husband feels far more intense than my feelings for my brother.

That thought makes me want to squirm, but I hold still. I don't want to disturb Colby. I did work him hard last night, it's only fair that I let him rest. Not moving a muscle for the entire journey is going to get uncomfortable, but I don't mind. Having a gorgeous young man snuggled up to me is hardly a hardship.

I let my mind drift as I savor the experience of Colby sleeping on me. By the time we arrive home, I am indeed very stiff. Colby stirs and his beautiful brown eyes regard me in sleepy confusion for a moment, before they widen in alarm.

"Oh gosh! Did I fall asleep on you?"

He looks horrified, as if it's the worst thing he has ever done. Knowing him, it could well be in his top five of most terrible acts. I can't fight the grin that stretches across my face.

"Please tell me I didn't drool on you! Or snore!" he exclaims.

I shake my head. He did a little of both, but I don't mind at all. It was incredibly endearing.

He bolts out of the car and I'm hit with a ridiculous amount of regret that I didn't get to open the door for him. What on earth has come over me?

It takes an embarrassing amount of time to climb out of the car and once I'm standing, I have to crick my neck. Colby is staring at me wide eyed. Clearly figuring out how stiff I am from being his personal mattress for hours.

"Do you want to come to my rooms? I can give you a massage?" He pauses and flushes a gorgeous shade of pink. "A normal, chaste massage."

I'm grinning again. I really hope that one day he offers me an abnormal, unchaste massage. That sounds delightful.

"I'm fine, besides, I'm sure you have things to do," I say.

He smiles at me and shrugs. "Not really. I was just going to catch up on the latest episode of The Last Of Us."

I ignore my pang of guilt at how empty his life is, now that he is wed to me and forced to fulfill a vessel's duty of lying around until he is ripe enough to surrender his magic to me. It's cruel and unfair. I'm sure Colby still has hopes, dreams and ambitions like everyone else. But I don't want to think about that right now.

"The one that came out last night?" I hazard a guess.

His eyes light up. "You've been watching it too?"

I nod, and he beams at me. It feels good to make him happy. It's a feeling that could become addictive. I've never even heard of this show he is talking about, but what is one little white lie to a prince of lies like me? It's worth it to make him happy.

He gives me a shy look and my heart beats faster.

"You, um could come to my rooms and we can watch it while I give you that massage?" he offers tentatively.

I'm nodding my agreement before I have even thought about it. I want to spend more time with him. There are things I need to do. But nothing that can't wait. I have a sinking feeling that even if they were urgent, I'd still neglect them in favor of basking in Colby's presence for a little longer.

The smile he gives me is truly dazzling. Its light reaches the darkest corners of my soul. I give him a grin in return and follow him to his rooms. I wonder if he knows that I would follow him to the ends of the earth?

Chapter Twenty-Two

Colby

A wide yawn overtakes me and a quick glance at the time shows me that I really need to stop falling down this rabbit hole of true crime videos on YouTube and go to sleep.

I guess Harry isn't coming to my room tonight, which is fine. The man probably needs a rest and my magic will never settle if we keep going at it like rabbits. A giggle escapes me but it is okay, there is no one here.

I love how physically intimate Harry and I have become. Now I just need to get him to talk to me. Open up and express feelings. I know it's going to take time. Harry is a British duke. Communicating his feelings isn't really in his wheelhouse. I'm going to have to teach him. And then everything is going to be wonderful.

Grinning, I close my laptop and pop it on the bedside table. Wriggling down into the comfy covers makes me feel all kinds of content. Life is good.

I drift off to sleep with a smile on my face, only to be awoken with a start by a hand over my mouth. My eyes fly open to find gray eyes staring down at me from a face framed by long blond hair.

"Eban?" I say in muffled bewilderment.

He smiles and removes his hand, freeing me to scramble up to a sitting position. My cousin is dressed all in black and inexplicably in my bedchamber in the middle of the night.

"What are you doing here?" I ask.

He rolls his eyes. "Rescuing you, you dolt!"

I can only stare. Rescuing me? From what? So slowly that it's almost painful, my stunned brain cells start to work. I used to think Harry was an asshole. I had been scared to marry him because of his reputation. His reputation of assaulting a vessel.

Eban, even though exiled from society and living with his bodyguard boyfriend, would have heard of my wedding. Eban, who is my friend. A friend I helped rescue from kidnappers. A friend who is far too kind to stand by while I am suffering.

Except I'm not suffering. Harry isn't evil or cruel. Just a little troubled.

"I don't need rescuing," I say numbly.

A cold breeze from my open window makes me shiver. Eban doesn't look convinced by my words. The only look on his face is one of pity.

"I'm sorry it took so long," he whispers. "But we need to go, right now."

He grabs my arm and pulls me out of bed and towards the window. I'm wearing my old comfy Star Wars pajamas and it's horribly embarrassing. I wouldn't have minded Harry seeing them, mostly because I suspect he would find them cute, but I don't want anyone else to see.

A head pops up in my window. Nearly frightening the life out of me, but then I recognize who it is.

"Bastion!" I squeal in delight.

"Hi, Kiddo," he grins.

Despite the circumstances, it's great to see Eban's bodyguard-turned-boyfriend. I'd love to have a catch-up and find out all about their new life together. I just need to get them to stop trying to steal me away in the middle of the night. But Eban is frightfully strong and is pulling me relentlessly towards Bastion, as much as I am trying to resist. I need to think of something to say, something that they will believe and not think is Stockholm Syndrome. And I need to think of it right now.

"Unhand my vessel," Harry's deep voice rumbles from behind me.

Oh crap, this isn't good. I don't want to be kidnapped, but I really don't want Harry to hurt my friends. Eban whirls, taking me with him. Harry is standing just inside my door. He is wearing gray pajama trousers and a dark silk robe. His wonderful chest is on display. Even in a time like this, it's very distracting.

Harry summons his magic, and I step in front of Eban. If everyone would just calm down for one minute, but Harry looks utterly wounded and betrayed by my protective gesture, and he lifts his hand to cast a spell, but then suddenly he crumples lifeless to the floor.

"Harry!" I screech, but Eban is holding me tight and won't let me go to him.

Someone else climbs through my window. Lord Garrington? The man whose vessel Harry attacked. This is the very opposite of good. Garrington strides over to Harry's helpless body.

"Leave him alone!" I try to say but no sounds come out of my mouth. Not content with knocking Harry out, the bastard has now put a silence spell on me!

"Now what do we do?" hisses Eban, sounding alarmed.

Garrington frowns as he looks down at Harry. "Take him with us."

"That wasn't part of the plan!" says Eban.

"This one being noisy and uncooperative wasn't part of the plan either," says Garrington with a shrug.

I've never been so indignant in all my life. Excuse me? Break into my bedchamber in the middle of the night and try to abduct me and somehow I'm at fault? I know they mean well, they think they are saving me. But honestly, the cheek of it.

"Bastion, you carry Sothbridge, and I'll carry Colby."

Since I can't talk, I struggle in Eban's grip as a way to express my displeasure at this plan. But he just makes soothing noises.

"I know it's overwhelming Colby, but we have got you now, everything is going to be okay. Nobody is going to hurt you anymore."

Hurt me? Oh lord, this is terrible. Please don't tell me my parents are involved in this misguided intervention. But I can just picture them telling Eban about my black eye.

I'm all out of options, I'm just going to have to go with them. Once we are wherever they are taking me, they will feel safe and calm down and remove this stupid silence spell. Then I will be able to talk and explain everything.

Bastion picks Harry up and throws him over his shoulder in a fireman's lift. I wince. These people hate Harry and he is completely vulnerable. Defenseless. No, not defenseless, he has me. I won't let them hurt him.

Lord Garrington strides towards me but I shake my head and dart to the open window before he can scoop me up. Eban's sigh of relief makes me feel all sorts of conflicted. As does voluntarily leaving with mine and Harry's abductors.

I can only pray that this disastrous misunderstanding is all sorted out soon and nobody is left with any hard feelings. But the look of betrayal on Harry's face before he went down, doesn't fill me with much hope. He is not a man who trusts easily. Will I ever be able to win it back?

My throat tightens. How has everything gone so wrong?

Chapter Twenty-Three

"I don't have Stockholm Syndrome!"

Saying it louder doesn't seem to convince Eban anymore than the thousand times I have said it quietly. I huff in frustration and cross my arms.

"I know it is confusing," Eban begins again.

"It's not confusing!" I interrupt. "Just because your husband was an asshole, doesn't mean that mine is!"

The flash of hurt on Eban's face makes me feel awful. He has gone to so much effort to help me, and as misguided as it all is, he does not deserve my rudeness.

"Sothbridge is not a nice person. He molested Fen and tried to claim him as his own. Xander had to fight him in a duel to stop him taking Fen away. He gave you a black eye. He flew into a rage at a ball, dragged you away and you weren't seen again for the rest of the evening. Just because you were dancing with someone."

I'm just staring at Eban. I know I am. But I can't find the words. Everything he said is true. Sort of. Just not in the way he is thinking.

"It's not like that," I mumble uselessly.

Harry had motives for trying to steal Lord Garrington's vessel. Not very nice ones and probably just revenge. But he had a reason. And my black eye was an accident, and at the ball he had been furious at Baxby, not me, but I don't really know why.

Even just saying it in my head, it doesn't sound very convincing. How the hell am I going to fix this? This first step of my plan - getting my friends to let me and Harry go, is turning out to be impossible. Nevermind the second step of talking Harry out of smiting everyone the moment he is free.

"Where is Harry?" I ask morosely.

"In the basement, warded and in magic binding cuffs. He is not getting free." Eban pats me reassuringly on my knee and pours some more tea.

The thought of Harry like that is as far from reassuring as it is possible to be. Is he scared? Furious? Does he think this was all my idea and that I have betrayed him?

"Can I see him?" I wince at how whiny I sound.

Eban shakes his head and hands me my refilled cup of tea. I take it and have a sip. It feels all kinds of wrong to be doing something so normal while Harry is imprisoned. I'm sitting here, in a lovely drawing room, while he is in a cold, dark basement. I can't stand it.

"What about when I am ripe?" I challenge.

Eban winces. "We thought of that, don't worry. Archie is hosting a small dinner party here tomorrow to introduce you to some nice mages."

I stare at Eban in horror, but he is deadly serious. He really just expects me to choose someone else to sleep with? As if it's nothing more than shopping for a new pair of shoes? He squirms uncomfortably under the force of my glare.

"I'm sorry, darling. I know it's not ideal. But Xander and Archie are very devoted to their boyfriends."

My tea goes everywhere. I can't believe Eban just said that. As if sleeping with Lord Garrington or Earl Hathbury would be any better.

Eban pats my back as I try to stop choking and compose myself. I can't help noticing he didn't offer his own boyfriend. And the thought of being intimate with Bastion makes me start coughing all over again.

I spent years of my life being a frustrated horn dog but now it seems I only want Harry. The idea of anyone else is beyond disgusting.

"Well, there is no point worrying about it now," says Eban brightly, but he is fooling no one. "You are not ripe yet, we can cross that bridge when we come to it."

A timid tap on the door seems to perk Eban up. Looks like he is glad for reinforcements.

"Come in!" he calls.

A young man slips in. He flashes me a quick glance before his gaze drops submissively to the floor. He really looks like he doesn't want to be here at all. I huff. Well, that makes two of us.

"Colby, this is Charlie Lidford, Archie's boyfriend."

Wait a minute. Is this Charles Lidford? The vessel that used to belong to Earl Rathbone before Earl Hathbury won him in a duel? And now he is in a relationship with Hathbury and not just his vessel? I hadn't heard that part.

I quickly assess the unassuming young man. He seems nice enough. Not particularly powerful. He doesn't seem the sort to inspire mages to duel over him.

"A pleasure to meet you, your Grace," he says softly.

"Likewise," I reply automatically.

"Come, take a seat!" says Eban, gesturing at an empty chair.

Charlie shuffles forward and tentatively sits, as if he thinks the furniture might rear up and bite him at any moment. Eban pours him a cup of tea and Charlie takes it with shaking hands. Is he always like this? Is it me? Do I scare him?

He used to belong to Earl Rathbone, the man I suspect traumatized Harry when he was a teenager. Is this what Rathbone does to people? I swallow over my dry throat.

"You used to belong to Earl Rathbone, didn't you?" I ask.

Charlie flinches as if someone struck him, and he hunches over. "Y... yes, that's right," he stammers. Eban glares at me.

"I find his alchemy work fascinating," I say. I need to know more about Rathbone, without giving away any of Harry's secrets. Especially as I only have suspicions at the moment. I have no idea how uncovering anything is going to get me out of this current mess, but it's worth a try.

Charlie somehow makes himself even smaller. He doesn't look at me as he speaks softly, but clearly.

"I'm afraid it was all far above my understanding, your Grace."

"I can relate to that!" I say cheerily. "What was he like to work with?" I ask, quickly followed by crying out "Ow!" as Eban kicks my ankle.

Charlie's gaze flies up to mine in alarm at my sudden exclamation. His deep brown eyes are beautiful. And the most haunted I have ever seen.

"Sorry, never mind me, I'm always one for making the conversation dull. Let's talk about something else," I babble as I try to backpedal.

Eban jumps in and starts talking about some crazy drama that recently happened in the wolf shifter pack he is living with. And I'm grateful for his save. I sip my tea and pretend to be paying attention.

I watch Charlie out of the corner of my eye and I'm relieved when he seems to relax. It's only a little, but he at least doesn't look as terrified as he did when I was talking about Rathbone. I feel like an ass for upsetting him, but at least now I know. Earl Rathbone is evil.

How I am going to use this information to my advantage, is another question entirely. But I'll think of something. I'm getting Harry out of here if it's the last thing I do.

Chapter Twenty-Four

The sound of soup spoons clanging against bowls fills the dining room. It makes me want to scream. I'm being held prisoner, but everyone is pretending I'm a guest. I don't even know Earl Hathbury and I have no idea how he was roped into hosting all of this. I glare at the young earl sitting at the head of the table, as if it is all his fault.

Eban and Bastion are sitting on the right-hand side of the table and Garrington and his fake-brother-turned-vessel on the left. But Charlie is nowhere to be seen. I thought he was the earl's boyfriend?

"Is Charlie well?" I ask.

Eban looks up at me. "He is fine, he just finds company difficult."

I huff, yeah I got that impression earlier. If he dislikes people so much, why did he bother joining us for tea? Unless... Oh gods don't tell me it was supposed to be some mistreated vessel solidarity. A support meeting of survivors. With tea.

I groan. I know Eban suffered at Hyde's hands and Charlie was clearly treated awfully by Rathbone. But I really, truly don't belong in that group.

Thinking of Rathbone causes my gaze to flick to Garrington. The son of the man who traumatized Charlie and I strongly suspect, hurt my husband. How does he fit into all of this?

"Or is Charlie avoiding you?" I ask pointedly.

Garrington puts down his spoon and fixes me with a steady stare.

"Well? He belonged to your father for years, lived in the same house as you. And clearly you did nothing."

A faint flush of color spreads across Garrington's face. "I got him away in the end."

I snort. "Too little too late."

Garrington's vessel is looking down at his lap, chewing his bottom lip and looking upset.

"I agree," says Garrington calmly.

I blink in surprise but like fuck am I backing down. "So now you go around rescuing vessels in an attempt to make amends."

Garrington's gaze is unflinching. "Yes," he replies simply.

I throw my napkin down in exasperation and lean back in my chair. "Would be a nice plan, if you rescued vessels who actually needed it!"

"Colby!" admonishes Eban.

But I don't care. I've been abducted. I'm allowed to be rude.

"One of us needs to deal with him," says Garrington. "Nobody else will be able to get here in time."

"Unless..." interjects Eban, before Hathbury interupt with a stern, "No."

Everyone squirms awkwardly. What the hell? Is Garrington threatening me? Talking about punishing me for being rude? How dare he!

A shiver rocks my body, hard enough to rattle my teeth. Then dizziness washes over me. Oh shit. Sudden realization hits me and it's like being punched in the gut.

I'm ripe. Very ripe. I don't think I've ever been so full of magic.

They were going to host the 'Pimp Colby Out' dinner tomorrow. I guess no one thought I was going to be ripe so soon. And right now the only mages here are the ones sitting around this table. Bastion is not a mage, but he is a shifter. His innate magic is enough to call out a vessel's. But I don't want him. I don't want any of them.

"Let me go to Harry," I say calmly.

Everyone looks at me in uncomfortable disbelief.

I grit my teeth. "Unless you want to rape me or let me explode and burn this house down, you don't have a choice!"

More uncomfortable squirming. Damn these people are annoying!

"For fuck's sake, he is chained up isn't he? He can't hurt me!"

Eban stands up. "Alright, I'll take you to him." He turns to face the murmurs of dissent. "Everything he said is true."

Finally. Finally someone is listening to me. I almost want to cry in relief. Instead, I climb to my feet and follow Eban to the basement.

The basement is very clean. It's warm and doesn't feel too damp. It is very dark though. There is an actual toilet and a small sink. A narrow single bed has been placed in the corner but Harry is sitting on the floor, his back resting against the bed, his cuffed and chained hands in his lap. His head is bowed as if he is regarding his restraints, and his golden hair gleams in the gloom.

My breath hitches at the sight of him. He is still dressed in the pajama trousers and gown he was captured in, and seeing him out of his impeccable suits makes him look so vulnerable.

Eban scurries away, locking the basement door behind him. Harry and I are alone.

Slowly he raises his head, the brightness of his aquamarine eyes is muted. "Come to mock me?"

My feet take me to him and I'm falling to my knees. I take his bound hands in my own.

"Harry, please believe me. None of this was my idea. I'm trying to talk sense into them. They think you have been mistreating me."

He is staring at me intently, as if he can read all my secrets in the irises of my eyes. He doesn't move. I'm not sure if either of us are breathing.

"Haven't I?" he asks softly.

I shake my head. "Well, taking me to that orgy wasn't great, but you saw the error of your ways."

A thousand emotions flash across his face but I can't name a single one of them.

"Why are you here?" he asks.

I feel my cheeks heat. "Isn't it obvious?"

His beautiful eyes narrow. "There are plenty of mages here, you don't need me."

"What part of me only wanting you, is so hard to understand?" I exclaim in exasperation. Why doesn't he believe me on this one simple matter?

"Nobody has ever wanted me before."

His words hit like punches. Spoken by someone else, they could so easily sound whiny or self-pitying. But he speaks them so calmly, so matter of fact. As if he is merely commenting on the color of the sky, and I can see the truth of them. People may have craved his wealth, his looks, his power. But nobody took the time to get to know him. To want Harry.

He speaks again. "I'm supposed to believe that you didn't plan my capture and that you are here now only because you are ripe and you don't want anyone else?"

I nod. Hopefully, he can see the honesty in my eyes, because I have no other evidence. No other way of convincing him.

He shakes his head gently. "You have no idea how much I want that to be true."

My heart clenches so tightly that I wonder if it is ever going to beat again.

Within me my magic flares impatiently. It doesn't care about trust or feelings. It simply wants to be free, and it knows Harry can provide that. It stokes my arousal and a helpless whimper escapes me.

Lust flares in Harry's eyes. Despite everything, he still wants me. I cling on to that hope with everything I have. If he refuses me, I... I can't even finish that thought. It's too awful.

Slowly, Harry lowers the waistband of his pajamas, just enough for his cock to spring free. It's nearly as hard as my own. I lick my lips.

"Is this what you want?" he whispers.

I nod and try not to drown in my own drool.

"Come and get it then," he says.

It's all the invitation I need. I lower my head and shove as much of his cock into my mouth as I can fit. He groans. The taste of him floods my mouth. All musky and masculine. He fills all my senses. I feast on him eagerly. The feel of him on my tongue is so familiar, it is a shock to realize I've never tasted him before. I've enjoyed the magic dildo, but never the real thing. I have to say, I'm a great fan of reality.

I slide down as far as I can, but pull up when I start to gag. One day I will take him all, I swear. I will just have to practice a lot. Like every day. Hopefully, he won't object to my plan.

I lose myself in the sensation of him as I hum my delight. The salty taste of his pre-cum is a whole new pleasure. One to add to my list of new favorite things.

"Colby!" he groans in warning.

Reluctantly I pause but I can't bring myself to release his cock from my mouth.

"Need to come inside you!" he gasps.

I want to taste all of him, but he is right. To take my magic, he needs to be inside me. Inside my ass, not my mouth. And now that I'm thinking of the feel of him stretching me wide, it seems like a wonderful idea. I let go of his cock with a loud plop, shove my trousers and underwear down to my mid thigh, and straddle his lap.

"Don't hurt yourself," he says, and his concern warms me.

I'm so very aroused, and his cock is wet from my mouth. I'm sure I will be fine. He loops his bound hands over my head, to encircle my back. I rise up on my knees and grab his cock with one hand to steady it. Carefully I line it up to my hole. Then slowly, I start to lower myself onto it.

It feels like being impaled. It's incredible. I like the burn, the sting, and as I sink further onto him, the feeling of fullness is bliss.

I sink all the way and groan. I love having Harry inside me and I don't think that's just the magic talking. I sit still for a moment, letting my body adjust. But I'm not feeling very patient at all.

My hands are on his shoulders, perfect for added leverage. I rise up a little and the drag is mind blowing. I sink back down and cry out.

"Alright?" asks Harry.

I can't open my eyes, so I nod frantically. "Very!"

He chuckles, and it reverberates through me, causing another wave of bliss. I rise up again and find a rhythm and angle that is ecstasy.

My head falls back as I revel in the joy of riding Harry. There is no blood in my veins, just euphoria.

"You are so beautiful," gasps Harry.

And just like that I peak. Pleasure, bliss and magic all roaring out of me with a scream that echoes around the walls.

Guess I have a praise kink. I sag against him, rest my head on his shoulder and let myself drift away. In this moment nothing else matters, save that I am in his arms. It is all that I need.

Chapter Twenty-Five

I'm still mostly soporific when Eban comes to fetch me. As soon as Harry hears him approaching, he pulls my trousers up for me and uses his strong hands on my hips to push me up to my feet. I don't want to leave him. I want to stay. His prison should be my prison. I shouldn't be sleeping in a lovely guest room, while he is down here, chained to the fucking wall. He has done nothing wrong.

But I'm too tired to yell at Eban. He knows my dream has always been to be a vessel and a good husband, and he thinks I am clinging onto that fairytale with everything I have and ignoring all the red flags. How do you convince someone who thinks you are deluded, that you are not deluded, if they think everything that comes out of your mouth is a delusion?

It's an impossible puzzle. I give Harry a forlorn look and he gives me the tiniest of smiles.

"I'm sorry," I say. "I will get you out of here soon."

He doesn't look like he believes me, and I can't say I blame him. I'm not the faith inspiring type. I'm just an ex-healer who likes getting railed, and drinking tea. Hardly a courageous warrior to have on your side.

Eban pulls me away and I shuffle after him. I'm still exhausted after giving up all my magic. And I really need a shower. Cunning plans are going to have to wait until tomorrow.

I give Harry one last lingering look, before the stairs hide him from view. Now I have to blink away my tears before Eban sees and blames Harry.

I have to think of a way out of this. I just have to.

After a good night's sleep, I wake up with sudden clarity. I clearly can't convince my well-meaning friends to let me and Harry go. So I need to give up on that and focus on escaping. One of them has the keys to the magic binding cuffs holding Harry. I just need to find out who, steal them and free Harry. Simple.

A groan of dismay escapes me. My history of enacting cunning plans successfully is exactly zero. Well, rescuing Eban worked well, but that plan had mostly been Bastion's. I merely played my part.

This time, it's just me, and this time I can't fail. I need to pull myself together. I can do this. I have to.

I hurry down to breakfast so I can start work on my plan. Eban is the only one in the breakfast room, a half-empty cup of coffee in front of him. I have a feeling he has been lingering with the intention of seeing me. Fine by me. It makes it easier for me to get to work. I don't think he has the keys, but I need to rule him out to be sure.

"Good morning, darling. How are you feeling?" he asks.

"Fine," I grumble while helping myself to some still warm toast.

A complete change of heart will be too suspicious. So I think I should aim for appearing grumpily resigned.

"I hated leaving you with him last night," Eban says softly and the guilt in his eyes tears at my heart. He is an infuriating ass, but he really does care.

"It's what I wanted," I state clearly.

He gives me a weak smile and looks slightly mollified. It will have to do. I can't wait until this is all over and everything is good between us. It's horrid being at odds with him.

I sit across from my cousin and spread marmalade on my toast and then take a big bite. It's delicious. But as lovely as breakfast is, I need to keep up my grumpy act.

"Have you remembered to feed Harry his gruel?" I snipe.

Eban sighs wearily. "We are treating him well. We are not monsters. Archie took him a proper breakfast. Everything we have here."

Archie. Earl Hathbury. Master of the house we are in. It would make complete sense if he was the one with the keys. I know someone will be keeping them. They'd hardly leave them on a handy hook by the basement door. They are not stupid.

"I hope you are not letting Garrington down there, given his history with Harry?" I ask.

"Of course not! What do you take me for?" says Eban.

It is strangely reassuring that he is not denying that Garrington would bear a grudge or take advantage of the situation. Eban's phrasing also implies that he is in charge here and it was all his doing. So maybe he does have the keys?

I huff as if I'm just annoyed. Silence falls as I eat my breakfast and Eban sips his coffee.

"Am I allowed to get some fresh air?" I whine and it's a little alarming that I'm so good at sounding petulant.

"I can walk around the gardens with you?" Eban offers.

Perfect. Exactly what I wanted him to say. We can stroll around the grounds and I can listen for the jingle of keys. I stuff the rest of my toast in my mouth and gulp down my tea. Eban finishes his coffee and we set off.

It's a lovely day, if a little chilly, and the gardens are stunning, even in the tail end of winter. In other circumstances, I would be really enjoying this.

I set a fast pace and I can't hear any jingling from Eban. But he is wearing tight jeans. If the keys are in one of those pockets, they wouldn't be moving at all. But in that case, surely there would be a clear outline.

The keys cannot be on his torso because he was wearing a tee shirt when we were at the breakfast table and he popped on a fluffy white jumper before we stepped outside. Neither of those will have pockets, so the keys have to be in his jeans. If he has them.

I risk trying to sneak a peek. Heaven help me if I'm caught, it's going to look like I'm checking out my cousin's ass or his crotch. He is a very good-looking man, but in a femme twink way. Not my thing at all. And, you know, my cousin! I'm not a pervert. At least, not that kind of pervert.

Okay, I need to stop this train of thought and concentrate. Keep my mind focused on the task at hand.

"Are you going to keep Harry locked up forever?" I hate to be so belligerent but I need a distraction.

Eban sighs despondently. "Of course not. The plan was never to capture him at all. We were just supposed to whisk you away."

I can hear the stress and worry in his voice. It makes me feel guilty. He got himself in this predicament in his desire to protect me. He is probably regretting everything.

"We will think of something," he says.

From his point of view, simply releasing Harry is not an option. Harry will be furious and either enact revenge or involve the mage council. Possibly both. An angry, powerful mage with connections, and the paranormal authorities, are both things I wouldn't want to have after me. Either separately or together.

Just what solution Eban and his little band are hoping for, I can't envision. So maybe, I can talk them into releasing Harry, after all? If I get Harry to swear there will be no consequences? That should encourage them. Thing is, can I get Harry to promise such a thing?

I sigh and rub my forehead. Why is everything so difficult?

Well, at least now I'm fairly certain that Eban doesn't have the keys. I've stolen a fair few glances at his butt and I can't hear any jingling. Now I need to somehow wrangle some time with Hathbury, to see if he has the keys. And then try to get someone to let me see Harry, to see if I can talk him into a truce. Since I might as well work on both plans at once.

I'm going to have a terrible headache by the end of the day, I can just tell. And that really is the very least of my worries.

Chapter Twenty-Six

At this rate, I'm going to grind my teeth down to stubs. Half an hour after finding Hathbury in the library, the man still hasn't moved from his desk. He is just sitting there, politely answering all my inane questions about the books lining the shelves. How am I ever going to find out if he has the keys?

Okay, take a deep breath. I can do this. I fall silent. Out of the corner of my eye, I see Hathbury's attention flick back to his computer screen. I quickly grab the most expensive looking book I can see and let it fall to the floor with a thud. It lands spread open on its front. I hope I haven't damaged it, it does look quite old.

Hathbury is by my side in an instant, squatting down to carefully retrieve the book, and gently smooth the pages back into place.

"Oh, I'm so terribly sorry!" I exclaim.

"It's quite alright," he says politely, but I can tell by the way his hand is shaking as he tries to straighten a crumpled page, that he is fuming.

I'm such an ass. Hathbury has risked so much to open up his home to harbor a stranger. Just from the kindness of his heart.

Just because he wants to save others from what his boyfriend suffered. And here I am trashing his books.

Shamelessly, my gaze flicks down to his pockets and I nearly squeal in delight. The way he is squatting has pulled a ring of keys halfway out of the pocket of his chinos. The keys are attached to a chain on his belt. The whole setup, with the size and shape of the keys, looks medieval, so unless he and Charlie are into kinky stuff, they have to be the keys to the magic binding cuffs.

A moment of doubt washes over me. It would just be my luck to steal the keys to someone's cock cage. Okay, no. I'm not thinking about that, thank you very much. I'm going to go with the assumption that these are the right keys.

Now I just need to work out how to steal them.

A surge of magic thrums like a shock wave through the library. A second later I hear the bang. What the hell is going on? Hathbury jumps to his feet and stares out of the window. He is distracted, this is perfect. Somehow, I reach out, unclasp the keys and shove them into my own pocket.

Suddenly, Hathbury turns on his heels and flees the library as if the hounds of hell are after him. Are we under attack? Nervously, I creep towards the window.

My mind goes blank as I stare at the sight before me. I cannot be seeing what I think I am seeing? Jem and several of Harry's staff standing in front of the house with a minivan behind them? As I watch, Jem throws a charm bag down onto the gravel drive and I feel the wards protecting the house start to disintegrate.

DUKE SOTHBRIDGE'S VESSEL

Jem has lost his mind. He is just a vessel. Buying some charm bags is not a way to fight two mages. And for all he knows, there may be dozens of mages in the house. But then again, how does he even know Harry is here? Maybe he does have a great plan and access to all the information he needs. And now I have the keys I can help.

I run as fast as I can to the basement and nearly fall down the stairs in my haste. I skid on my knees across the floor to Harry and frantically start trying to unlock the cuffs. I can sense Harry's astonishment, but I haven't got time to feel hurt by that.

"Jem is here!" I gasp.

"Where?" demands Harry.

"Out the front, with some of our staff. He is throwing charm bags at the wards and it's working."

The cuffs click and then fall away. Harry jumps to his feet and pulls me with him. Then we are running. Up the basement stairs, along hallways and out to the front of the house. Someone flings magic at us but Harry deflects it without breaking his stride.

We've reached Jem. I'm trying to catch my breath, but Harry isn't ruffled at all. Fit as well as good-looking, aren't I lucky.

"I'm not strong enough to fight Garrington, let alone him and Hathbury," he tells Jem.

Jem gives him an intense look. "That was before you had a vessel, you are stronger now."

I feel a surge of pride, but Harry shakes his head. "It's not worth the risk. We need to flee."

He moves his hand and I feel his magic surge as he starts to cast. In no time at all a swirling orange portal opens. The heat and wind from it is intense. I feel my mouth drop open in astonishment. I had no idea that Harry was powerful enough to create portals.

"Everyone in!" orders Harry.

I have a moment to think of the minivan being abandoned and then Harry is pulling me into the portal. A few seconds of tumbling through time and space, like being on the world's most intense roller coaster, and we stumble out into Harry's study. Back in Stourleat House. Home.

I've landed on top of Harry and we are sprawled on the floor, but I can't move. I don't want to move. I wrap my arms around him and cling to him. It's over. He is free. Harry is safe. I'm so relieved. I think I am going to cry. Oh, I am crying.

Harry says something to Jem and climbs to his feet with me in his arms. I snuggle in even more and sob harder. Everything had been so awful, with seemingly no way out, and now like a miracle, everything is perfect. Harry is free, and no one has been hurt. At least, I don't think anyone has been hurt. I hope Eban and his little band are all okay.

Harry starts to carry me somewhere. My room? I don't care. Harry can take me anywhere. I am his. He is my everything. I really should stop crying, he was the one that was locked in a basement. I should be comforting him.

He places me in my bed. It's so very good to be home. I hope he climbs into my bed with me. I can make him forget all about being held captive. Well, have fun trying to, at least.

Jem walks in and I hope he just needs to check his brother is okay before leaving us alone. That would be fair enough. I take a deep breath and close my eyes. I need to get control of myself, this is embarrassing.

Harry's hands stroke my neck, then a loud click echoes around the room. My eyes fly open and my hands fly up to my throat. An iron collar. Harry has put an iron collar around my neck. My gaze tracks the attached chain all the way to the enormous, ancient and very solid radiator. I'm not going anywhere. Unless Harry allows it.

Betrayal claws through me and it fucking hurts. Now I can truly relate to how Harry must have felt. Like his soul was being ripped out. Ripped out, torn to shreds, set on fire and stomped on.

My gaze finds his. He looks conflicted and pained, but very, very resolute.

"It wasn't my idea," I say hoarsely. Surely he knows that? In his heart, if nothing else? "I came and unchained you!" I plead. That has to be all the evidence that he needs.

Harry winces. "After Jem had already started his attack. I felt the magic blasts."

I know I'm just staring helplessly but all the words I have ever learned have deserted me. I am no longer capable of speech. I'm drowning in the force of his aquamarine eyes. He suspects I am some sort of double agent. Pretending to be on his side because it suits my nefarious goals.

"I want to trust you Colby, but I can't risk my people. So until I know for certain where your loyalty lies, I need to take precautions."

Keeping me chained to a bed is a precaution? Precaution from what? I'm hardly dangerous. I mean, look at me. But I suppose I could be a spy, a mole or a saboteur. My heart sinks. He is not crazy to lock me up. Even if for no other reason than to use me as a bargaining chip against Garrington and Hathbury. Or to stop me being stolen again.

Harry turns to Jem. "We need to talk about how you found me, and where you got those charm bags from."

Jem gives me a conflicted, but cold glance and nods at his brother. Together they turn and walk out of my room. Leaving me alone. Alone and chained to a bed.

Great. Just great.

How am I going to get out of this one?

Chapter Twenty-Seven

It's far too quiet in my room. It is as if the loneliness is pressing in, mocking and cruel. Weighing down on my chest and making it hard to breathe. My husband hates me. My friends probably do too, after my betrayal. If not, they can never reach me. Harry will be on high alert now, the wards will be iron tight.

I also doubt he will let my parents anywhere near me. If I suspect their involvement, Harry will. He is not daft.

There is no hope. Harry is my husband and my master. If he wants to keep his vessel chained up, that is no one's business but his own. No one is coming to save me. I'm all alone.

It's a horrid, soul destroying feeling. I want to scream, to cry, but the motivation to do anything has been leached out of me until all I can do is lie here listlessly.

The thing that hurts the most is the thought of Harry despising me. It is the worst thing ever. I was so hopeful that our marriage was going to be a happy one. Everything had been going well, until it all went so wrong.

The door opens. Despondently, I look over. It's Harry, with a tray and a bucket. I scramble up to a sitting position, my heart beating like crazy. He didn't need to come himself. This is hopeful.

He sets the bucket by the wall and the tray of delicious smelling food on the bedside table. He doesn't look angry. Maybe he doesn't hate me and really is just being cautious.

"Are you alright?" he asks.

I think that is genuine concern in his eyes. I swallow. Letting hope bloom feels so dangerous. I'm not sure I can survive it being crushed. It would destroy me.

"I need the toilet," I say.

His gaze flicks to the bucket so I put on my best puppy dog eyes. He had access to a proper toilet when he was chained up. He stares at me for a moment before sighing.

"I won't make a run for it," I promise.

To my surprise, he chuckles. "I've seen you run, I'm not worried."

And indignant "Hey!" escapes my mouth before I can stop it.

He smiles. "You are very adorkable, Colby."

My heart flutters. Adorkable. I can live with that. I don't think I'm truly a dork. I'm neither clever nor clumsy enough. Though I do always seem to be very uncoordinated around him. I can't blame him for forming that opinion of me.

I should think of a witty and cute response, but the moment has passed and now he is unlocking the chain from the radiator.

"Go on, go use the bathroom before your food gets cold."

I don't need any further encouragement to scurry to my ensuite, trailing my chain behind me like some kind of ghost.

Pulling it in after me feels all kinds of awkward. Once it is all in, I push the door closed but don't lock it. I think that's a sign of good faith. An indication that I don't have secrets to hide and I'm not up to no good. And that I trust Harry not to peek.

I feel much better after using the facilities. I wasn't lying about my need and the need had been quite pressing.

As I'm washing my hands, I consider that being chained via a collar is much more convenient than having cuffed hands. The snort laugh that escapes me, startles another laugh out of me. I am laughing alone in the bathroom like a maniac and Harry can probably hear me.

I pull myself together and walk back out to my bedchamber. Harry has set up the food on the small two-seater table by the window and he is sitting on one of the chairs. He is eating with me?

I take my seat and survey the salmon and asparagus pasta. Dinner, I guess? It's alarming to realize how much I have lost track of time. It must be dinnertime, the same day we escaped from Hathbury House. It feels like I was chained alone in here for all eternity. It's mind boggling to think that it has only been a few hours.

I'm going to truly lose my mind if Harry keeps me in here for any length of time. But he is dining with me, so maybe my captivity will not last for long.

"This is nice," I say cautiously.

Harry looks pained. "It's not my intention to make you suffer, Colby."

I'm very glad to hear that. I flash him a smile and tuck into dinner. He has even poured some white wine. If I ignore the collar around my neck, this could be lovely. This will be lovely, because I am going to make it so.

"The weather has been lovely for this time of year," I say.

Harry barks out a laugh. "You are full of surprises."

"There is nothing surprising about wanting to enjoy a pleasant dinner with my husband," I reply and I take a sip of my wine. It is delicious.

Harry is staring at me intently. I meet his gaze evenly. I have nothing to hide. The air between us thickens. He really is incredibly good looking. Thank heavens for arranged marriages because I never would have got someone like him to even look at me, let alone marry me, in the outside world.

"I can't believe that anyone is as lovely as you appear to be," he says softly, as if he thinks saying it out loud will cause it not to be true.

I shiver. Poor Harry. I'm not lovely. I'm just perfectly normal. It says a lot about the backstabbers and vipers he has in his life, if he thinks I'm special.

"I'm just too daft to be devious," I say dismissively. "I'm not bright enough to have grand ambitions. All I have ever wanted is a husband, a mage to give my magic to."

Harry's look is considering. He is not rejecting my statement completely. Hopefully, he will see the truth of it.

"And I like you, Harry. A lot."

He scoffs and looks embarrassed. As if he doesn't know how to handle the compliment. To be fair, I'm not sure I would be able to either. But I hope he believes me.

"So, your friends thought I was mistreating you, came to rescue you and you knew nothing about it?" he asks and I can hear the disbelief in his voice.

"It's true," I say. "Garrington really hates you. Eban's husband was awful, so he thinks all mages treat their vessels appallingly. Charlie was cruelly mistreated. That all clouded their judgment."

Harry winces. "Eban has personal reasons to dislike me."

I drop my fork. Eban's husband used to share him out, I know that. Hyde is a close associate of Harry. I've just been burying my head in the sand by not connecting the dots before. Misery washes over me.

"I told you that I wasn't a nice person," Harry says sadly.

I take a deep breath. "Were you cruel? Did you hurt him? Scare him?"

"Not on purpose."

He looks so sad. Truly remorseful.

"It's not my crime to forgive," I say carefully.

"I know," he replies easily.

An uneasy silence falls between us. Steering the conversation away feels dismissive. Lingering on it seems unnecessary. My mood is plummeting into dark depths.

"I didn't realize that he didn't want to," Harry says, almost desperately.

I look up at him in surprise and he looks away uncomfortably and gives a small, awkward shrug. "Apparently, I cannot bear you thinking badly of me."

Then why tell me dark things? I nearly say, but I don't. I like him being honest with me. I don't want there to be secrets between us.

"I've been reading about that consent word you shouted at me in the library," he says. "It's not a concept I was familiar with, to my shame." He takes a deep breath. "It's not a courtesy that was afforded to me when I was young, so I did not know to extend it to others."

He comes to a shuddering halt. He is not looking at me and his shoulders are drooped. Is he telling me what I think he is telling me? Is that what Rathbone did to him? I reach out and place my hand over his. He exhales heavily.

"I have done wrong to so many. I completely mishandled what happened to Jem. I have not treated you well."

My heart is beating like crazy. I've known men raised like Harry, my whole life. I know how very hard it is to say all this, and I'm touched that he is willing to do so for me. Just because he can't bear the thought of me thinking poorly of him.

"I forgive you, for the mistakes you made with me," I say earnestly as I give his hand a little squeeze.

He looks up at me and the yearning I see in his eyes steals my breath away. He looks so much younger. More vulnerable than I have seen him before. It feels like I am looking at the real Harry. The man behind the walls and armor and the trappings of rank.

"I can't let you go," he whispers. "Not until I know for sure."

I nod at him.

"Hathbury belongs to an opposing political faction. I have to be sure it was nothing to do with that," he clarifies.

My eyes widen. Was there a political motive that I'm oblivious to? It hurts a little to think that helping me was just a cover, but I'm not so naïve as to dismiss the idea.

My mind whirls. I know Harry is a Revivalist, does that mean that Hathbury is an active Anti? Or is there a completely separate political difference between them? I have no idea. And I'm not even supposed to know about the Revivalist stuff.

"I understand," I say calmly.

I take a bite of the rapidly cooling dinner. I feel bad for not confessing what I know, but I want Harry to trust me, not grow more wary.

"How are you so damn nice?" asks Harry, sounding equal parts baffled and bemused.

"Just fell from heaven this way," I say with what I hope is a cheeky grin.

He laughs and my heart skips a beat.

"But you did fall?" he asks and his eyes flash with clearly naughty thoughts.

"I most certainly did," I agree, as I feel tingly all over.

He turns his attention to his lunch and I feel a flare of jealousy. I want his attention on me. I want the heat of his gaze. I want his hands all over my body.

I swallow over my suddenly dry throat. I'm not ripe. Just suddenly horny. I wonder what having sex with a collar on would be like. Gosh, I need to stop that train of thought. My cheeks are heating. Thank heaven's Harry is looking at his food. Seems it is a good thing after all.

"Have you received your invitation for the king's coronation yet?" I ask.

A nice safe topic of conversation. Even I can't turn this one filthy.

Harry nods. "Our invitation," he corrects.

I swallow. I hadn't been sure if news of our wedding would have reached the palace officials in time for their planning. Well, I guess that means Harry will have to release me before May. Since I cannot exactly attend the coronation in chains.

That's something to look forward to.

Chapter Twenty-Eight

Harry

I'm pacing my study like a madman but I can't stop. I despise that I'm showing Greyfield and the others how rattled I am, but not even that loathing is enough to still my limbs. Agitation and anxiety is flowing through my veins and any moment now I'm going to scream and scream and not be able to stop.

"Are you sure there was nothing in Hathbury's basement?" Greyfield asks.

I grind my teeth. "Quite sure."

My magic had been bound by the cuffs but I would have been able to sense a portal of the magnitude we had been hoping for. Whatever the cause, getting access to the basement of Hathbury House was a blessing in disguise. Either Hathbury does not know I'm a Revivalist or he is a cocky little shit. Rubbing it in that he did actually manage to destroy the portal.

Greyfield sighs heavily. I can taste his and everyone else's bitter disappointment. We had all been hoping that the destruction of the portal was all just an elaborate bluff and that portal was still growing. This news sets us back hundreds of years.

I growl in frustration. What the fuck is wrong with Hathbury? His grandfather was a genius. If the portal had been left to grow as per the plan, the Fey would have been able to cross it in a few decades.

"Did they take you just to gloat?" someone asks.

Fuck if I know. I let the conversation wash over me. I almost don't care. The only thing I do care about is Colby's innocence. He is innocent in all of this. I am sure of it. Aren't I?

I stop my frantic pacing just long enough to pour myself a whiskey and down it. The burn does nothing for me. It is as if I'm numb to it. Too full of pain to be able to register any more.

The image of Colby's beautiful brown eyes is haunting me. I can't stop thinking about his dazzling smile, his sweetness. The feel of him in my arms. He is the brightest thing in my life. It can't be nothing more than a mirage. That would break me.

"What does your vessel know?" asks Greyfield.

"Nothing," I croak. Gods, I hope it's true.

"Is that what you think? Or what you know?"

I wince. "There is no evidence that he knows a thing."

"Is there any evidence that he doesn't?"

Murmurs of conversation wash over me. I let them debate it without me. I've said all I can. Presented the facts as I know them. There is nothing more I can do. It is out of my hands now.

"It's quite clear. The boy needs to be put down. We can't take the risk."

I whirl to face Greyfield. Sparks ignite in between my fingers and rage flows through me. Greyfield pales and steps back.

"He is a good-looking boy and shaping up to be a powerful vessel. I agree it is a shame, but we can't take the risk. There is too much at stake, we don't know what he may have uncovered."

I ball my hands into fists and keep them clenched by my side. I'm not shocked by Greyfield's words. They were exactly what I was expecting.

"Of course, The Circle will compensate you for your loss. You'll be able to buy another vessel."

The words feel like a slap. They are exactly how I should feel about Colby. He is a vessel. Property. Something to be bought, sold and replaced. It's how I expected to feel about him.

I don't understand why I don't feel that way. How did he seep into my every pore and take up residence in my soul? It doesn't make any sense. He is cute, sweet, clever. Fantastic in bed. None of those are reasons to lose my frigging mind. But I have. Completely and utterly. And I have no idea what to do about it.

"He knows nothing," I assert.

Greyfield's eyes narrow. "Well, let's put it to the vote, shall we?"

I glare at each of the seven people in the room but I'm all out of words. I have nothing rational to add, because there is nothing rational to add. *Please don't kill my vessel who may be a spy and saboteur and may destroy us all. Don't kill him because I love him and it will break my heart.* Those words make no sense at all. Voicing them will only serve to let them know that I have completely lost the plot.

"All in favor of execution, raise your hand."

Like a nightmare or a vision of hell, I watch as one after another, seven hands raise up into the air. I can't breathe. My heart is exploding. My vision swims.

Greyfield pats me on the shoulder. "Sorry, Old Chap. We will make it quick and painless."

"No," I say.

Greyfield raises an eyebrow.

"No," I say again.

More sure this time. More sure than I have ever been of anything in my entire life.

"No." The third and final time feels like a charm.

Magic explodes out of me in a great glittering arc as I cast a binding net over everyone in the room. Their shrieks of shock and outrage are like music to my ears. Quickly, I ignite the sigils carved into the wall of my study and tether the net to their power.

Fighting seven other mages at once would be ludicrous if I wasn't in my own home, in my own study. Even so, I'm not going to be able to hold them for long.

I run as fast as I can to Colby's room and fling the door open with a force that startles Colby into jumping out of bed. I stride up to him, fumbling with the keys as I go. When I reach him, it takes an excruciatingly long time to get my hand to coordinate and get the key in the lock and turned. Finally, the collar falls away.

Colby is staring up at me with his big brown eyes.

"Run!" I plead. "Run and run and never look back. Change your name and never contact any Old Blood ever again. Trust no one."

His eyes grow even wider and his face drains of all color.

I growl in frustration, grab his arm and march him out of the room. I drag him down the hallway, to the nearest exit. I can feel my net disintegrating in the study under the force of seven mages working together. My pace increases. I'm not even sure if Colby's feet are touching the ground.

Somehow I get him outside. The gravel of the driveway crunches under me as I take Colby to the wooded area to the side of the house.

"Flee!" I urge him, giving him a shove towards the woods.

He stumbles and turns to face me.

"Please Colby!" I beg. "There is no time! Run! Run and live!"

His face is a mixture of shock, horror and confusion. But he nods and finally, finally he runs. I watch him go for a brief moment, then I turn and stride back to the house and my foes. I don't expect to survive this battle, but that's fine. I'm not the one that needs to.

As long as Colby lives, that is all that matters.

Chapter Twenty-Nine

Colby

I'm tripping over every stick, root and slight incline in these blasted woods. My knees and palms are covered in mud and I'm not getting very far.

Harry's terrified face haunts me, urging me on. What the hell is going on? I have no idea. But I know my life is at stake, that much is clear and that knowledge is keeping my feet moving.

Suddenly, a green portal opens up before me and I tumble through it with a shriek, and find myself in what looks like Hathbury House. Hathbury's study maybe? Eban, Bastion, Garrington and Hathbury are all grinning at me.

"You escaped! Well done, darling!" beams Eban.

I must have staggered past the wards protecting Stourleat House, enabling my friends to open a portal and grab me. I fall to my knees. I'm breathing like a steam train. My mind is spinning. My friends care enough to spend the vast amount of power it takes to open a portal. It should be flattering, but my husband's words are ringing in my ears.

Trust no one. Harry said. Have no contact with Old Blood. Change your name. Live.

I stare at the people surrounding me. I feel safe, but am I? Can I trust them? I have zero clue what is going on. What do I do? Can I really just leave Harry? And Jem and the staff, to whatever the hell is going on?

I don't think I'm the only one who is in danger, because that doesn't make any sense. Besides, the last look in Harry's eyes had looked far too much like farewell.

I whimper. I can't leave Harry to his fate, I can't. But can I get these people to help me? Or at least send me back?

"Please" I rasp out. "Please help them!"

I watch as the faces around me fill with concern and alarm. This wasn't what they were expecting when they sensed me stagger outside Harry's wards. It's a little reassuring. It seems like they aren't part of whatever is going on.

"What happened?" asks Eban.

I stammer my way through an explanation of Harry bursting into my room, the words he said and the way he dragged me out of the house. I even add in about him chaining me because he was worried about political repercussions. That won't endear him to them, but it might help them put together the puzzle pieces that I cannot begin to fathom.

Hathbury turns to Garrington. "Sounds like Sothbridge is turning against The Circle."

Eban looks as confused as I am. A vague memory teases at me. I think The Circle are an old and powerful Revivalist cult. It doesn't suddenly explain why my life is in danger.

"They probably thought Colby was an agent," Garrington says to Hathbury.

Hathbury pales. "I suppose our abduction of Sothbridge does look rather sinister."

Will somebody please start saying words that make sense? Please? Or better still, can we please go back to Stourleat and make sure Harry is okay?

In the end I think they agree to go out of curiosity more than anything. Hathbury whips out his phone saying something about back up. Garrington opens up a portal. Eban stands behind me and places his hands on my shoulders. I'm supposed to stay here, in safety. But I can't do that. Even though it is what Harry wants for me. I can't abandon him, I can't.

I wait until the two mages have stepped through and then just before the portal closes, I twist out of Eban's grip and dive through it. I land on my face in the woods. As I had hoped for, the slight time lag present in most portals means that Hathbury and Garrington are nowhere in sight. They can't stop me or send me back if they don't know I'm here.

It takes me a few moments to get my bearings and then I'm off. Stumbling through the woods, towards the house. I can only pray that Hathbury and Garrington will keep whatever trouble there is at bay, or at least distracted, so I can slip in.

As I approach the house, everything seems eerily quiet and still. Just a late afternoon in early spring. Soft, muted sunlight and no signs of life. I swallow over my tight throat and creep in. Even though I'm quite sure my heart is beating loud enough to herald my presence.

Is everyone dead? No! I can't let myself think that. I have to stay calm and rational. Even though being here isn't rational at all. I'm just a vessel, what can I do? But I have to try. I have to. I got help, I've been sensible. Now it is time to follow my heart.

My feet take me to Harry's study. The door is open. It's never open. I tiptoe in. Harry is sprawled on his back on the floor. I clamp my hand over my mouth to contain my scream. I'm by his side in an instant. His pulse is weak and reedy, but it is there, and I've never felt anything more beautiful. His breaths are far too shallow. His life force a faint, flickering thing. He has been utterly drained of magic. Almost to the point of death.

A soft whimper escapes me. There is no healing that can fix this. He needs magic and he needs it now. I have plenty, even though I was emptied not that long ago. I just don't have a way of giving it to him. It's not like he can fuck me while he is unconscious.

A blast of magic rocks the house. There is a fight going on somewhere. If any enemies come across Harry like this, he is done for. I wanted to help and here I am, I bloody well need to do something.

His too-pale, too-slack face makes my heart clench. Seeing him like this is far beyond awful. I can't stand it. I need to see his aquamarine eyes, his naughty, sardonic grin. I need to see him full of life and filling the room with his presence. He can't fucking die in my arms. I won't allow it.

I put my hands on the center of his chest, as if I'm about to do CPR. I can feel his essence. It's so familiar to me, so intimate. His essence has been wrapped around my own whilst our bodies

DUKE SOTHBRIDGE'S VESSEL 171

have been joined. I've felt my magic flow into him. Leaving me gladly, for someone who can actually wield it.

My magic stirs, it recognizes the feel of Harry. "Go on," I encourage it as I imagine my magic pouring out of me, down my arms and into him. A more intense version of healing someone. I've coaxed tendrils of magic into other people before, and guided it to knitting bones and so on. Surely this isn't so different?

But nothing is happening. In frustration, I lean down and press my lips against his. The familiar taste of him connects something within me and suddenly it is like a bridge is formed between us. My magic sees its chance for freedom and it flows. Like water over a broken dam. It rushes out of me, and into him. Fueling his flickering life force into a bright, steady flame.

Oh my god, it is working, it is actually working. I am doing it! Giddying excitement threatens to loosen my concentration, so I grimly set that emotion aside.

I'm so deep in what I am doing, that I don't see or hear someone enter the study, I sense it. It's somebody whose magic is a cacophony of different colors. This person has drunk from many different vessels, and often. There is a strand that feels like Jem and my stomach heaves.

I open my eyes. It's Lord Greyfield. Pasty Lord Greyfield who looks like a snake and who stole Harry away for business at the ball.

Is he a friend or a foe?

I don't know.

His cold eyes give nothing away. He strides towards me, yanks me away from Harry and wraps his hands around my throat and squeezes tightly.

Well, that answers that question, I think as I wheeze. I try to fight him off but he uses magic to keep me still. Coward. He clearly deems using magic to kill me outright is a waste, but he is not above using some to make this easy for him.

I don't want to die like this. I don't want to die at all, but certainly not like this. Maybe Harry will wake up and save me? No, I know he is still far too gone for that. I need to save myself.

But how?

His multicolored magic brushes against me, keeping me still but also connecting us. The strand that once was Jem's pulses. It has a familiar feel to Harry's magic. A familial connection, I guess. It seems to recognize me too.

I literally have nothing to lose, so it's worth a go. I call it to me. I'm a vessel, I naturally absorb magic from my surroundings. I've never tried absorbing it from a person before. I don't think anyone has tried this. But surely it is not that different?

Concentrate, I need to concentrate.

Suddenly it's like the sun has burst out of the clouds, and everything is clear. I can see how to do it. I call Jem's magic to me and it surges. It's twisted and tangled with all the other magic and it drags it along with it. Magic often acts like a liquid and I have created a siphon.

It pours out of Greyfield and into me. Potent and powerful and far too much. It is going to overwhelm me, consume me. But wait, I'm still connected to Harry. With a deep breath, I direct all the magic to Harry until I'm just a conduit. The magic flowing through me. Passing through me on its journey.

Until there is none left. Blearily I open my eyes. Greyfield is motionless on the floor. Harry is sitting up and gasping for air.

DUKE SOTHBRIDGE'S VESSEL 173

I'm about to crawl over to him but Garrington and Hathbury walk in. Harry tries to scramble to his feet and the panic in his face breaks my heart.

"It's okay Harry!" I call out. "They are on our side."

Harry stills, but eyes the mages warily and dubiously.

Hathbury and Garrington stare at Greyfield sprawled motionless on the floor, then at Harry, then finally at me. I feel the questioning brush of their magic as they try to decipher what the hell happened.

"Did you take Greyfield's magic and give it to Sothbridge?" asks Hathbury, sounding both surprised and a little awed.

I nod. I guess I should feel immensely proud of myself. But I only feel dazed. Is this what being in shock feels like?

"Impressive," remarks Garrington.

"Where are the others?" asks Harry. He sounds a little dazed too. I hope he is okay.

"The Circle have been defeated," says Hathbury.

"I'm assuming you have decided to leave them?" asks Garrington dryly.

Harry blinks, rubs his hands over his face. "I guess attacking them does count as a resignation." Then he huffs out a laugh.

I throw myself onto him, landing on his lap and forcing an "Oof" out of him. My arms wrap around his neck and I bury my head into his shoulder and breathe in his scent. His arms encircle my back and hold me tightly.

"You saved me," he says.

"You saved me first," I say.

He chuckles, "I guess that makes us even."

I shake my head, "Not until you kiss me."

"Seems fair enough," he says with a truly naughty grin.

Suddenly I'm on my back on the floor and Harry is over me. He leans in and his lips attack my own. The kiss is fierce, passionate, possessive and utterly wonderful. It ignites my desire and makes my toes curl. My arms are clinging onto him and I'm whimpering and moaning. My body rising up to meet his.

He breaks away and stares down at me with something that looks an awful lot like adoration in his stunning eyes. It makes my stomach flip over and my heart flutter. I cast a quick glance around the room.

"We scared Garrington and Hathbury away."

Harry grins, "Good."

And then he kisses me again.

Harry is quite right. Life is good.

Chapter Thirty

One Month Later

Harry is looking so devilishly handsome tonight that it is frightfully distracting. So much so that I nearly forgot to gesture for the staff to bring in the next course. That would have been a disaster for hosting my first formal dinner party.

I manage to pull my gaze away from my husband to look around the dining room and check my guests are happy. Eban is laughing at something Bastion said and I can just tell they are holding hands under the table. My parents are deep in conversation with Hathbury. Charlie is sat between his boyfriend and Eban, his two favorite people, and it seems to be working, he doesn't look too terrified.

Jem is next to Harry, with my parents on his other side. He seems engrossed in listening to their conversation. He is doing well for his first social engagement as an adult. I do really hope I can wrangle more for him.

Denise and her lovely wife are next to me.

It's a shame Garrington and his vessel declined but I understand. Burying the hatchet as they say, is one thing. A dinner party with your former foe is quite another.

But everyone who is here looks happy. My mother's insistence that the key to a good dinner party is good wine, appears to have paid off. My gaze flicks back to Eban. He has poured himself a third glass of the alcohol-free wine that I hunted high and low to find. I'm so relieved. Finding one that actually tasted decent was certainly a challenge.

I look back at Harry, sitting at the head of the table, opposite me. His eyes are fixed on me. Everyone around us is chatting. A sea of noise and movement. A room full of people, but we steal this private moment. He gives me a naughty wink, sips his wine and turns his attention back to his guests, like the good host that he is.

I won't be ripe for another three days but that doesn't stop my arousal from flaring. I can't wait to get my hands on him tonight. And I know he won't mind at all.

I take a sip of wine to hide my filthy grin. I might actually keel over from happiness and die. Everything, absolutely everything is perfect. I know there will be rumblings from Revivalists for years. But I'm confident that Harry and his new allies can handle anything that is thrown our way. Revivalist idiots have been a thorn in society's side for hundreds of years, nothing has changed there. Except that Harry is no longer one of them.

Because he chose me.

My heart flutters like crazy. As it does every time I think of it. How romantic can you get? My husband is the most romantic man in the entire universe.

Dinner finishes far too soon, but we move to the parlor and the conversation continues to flow. I drift around and make sure to talk to everyone. Jem seems to really hit it off with Eban and they are soon laughing about something. The sight fills me with joy. Though I shouldn't be surprised, they are both flamboyant, confident and gorgeous. It's not surprising that they'd get along.

I check on Charlie and Hathbury, and Charlie gives me a shy smile. I don't think he is completely hating the evening, which makes me want to burst with pride.

Harry sits at the piano and an expectant hush falls. The first few notes flow out and dance along my spine, making me shiver. He is an excellent pianist. Really, really good. He looks so happy playing as well. I need to encourage him to do it more often.

We spend most of our nights in my room, but I have seen his a few times now. The sheer amount of instruments strewn everywhere, tells me that it's not just the piano that he plays. He doesn't need to hide his passion away. I want to hear him. I want everyone to hear him.

Time in jovial company passes swiftly, but soon I'm hiding my yawns. Hathbury and Charlie retire first and I have a moment of panicking if their room is good enough. Even though I inspected it myself. Several times. I know it's perfectly clean and that they have everything they need to be comfortable.

I suppose Hathbury could open a portal and whisk them home if they really hate it, but it would be a frightful waste of magic and I truly hope they don't feel the need.

Taking a deep breath, I make myself stop fretting and turn my thoughts to magic instead. I'm fascinated by the knowledge that vessels can pass on magic without intercourse. I'm not even annoyed that Eban and the others knew but thought I shouldn't know. It is a dangerous secret. All powerful ones are.

But now Harry and I are in this top secret club, they have been very willing to share all they have learned about it. I still can't get over the fact that it was timid little Charlie that discovered it. He is not keen on experimenting any further, but that's fine, because I am very willing to. As is Harry. I never thought I'd be interested in magical research! But such is life. Always full of surprises.

Another yawn overtakes me. I can't hide them anymore. I walk over to Harry who is sitting on a settee with my parents and discussing Beethoven.

"I'm going to retire," I say.

He starts to rise but I stop him by leaning down and giving him a quick kiss on the cheek. "Enjoy the rest of your evening," I say.

He smiles at me, takes my hand and brings it to his lips for a kiss. "Goodnight."

I grin soppily all the way to my room.

A quick shower and then I dive under the sheets. Naked. Because I'm sure Harry won't be long. He never is. And now I'm in the comfort and solitude of my own room, my tiredness has vanished. Replaced by excited anticipation. I'm sure it's the effect of my subconscious connecting being in bed with very naughty things. Really can't blame my subconscious for making that connection. It has an awful lot of evidence to go on.

I lie back and get comfy and wait.

And wait. And wait some more. The distant sound of the piano drifts up to me. I frown. Really? He really wants to play piano more than he wants to be up here ravishing me?

Huffing in displeasure, I roll on to my side and reach into my bedside cabinet to retrieve the magic dildo. I'll just have to remind him what he is missing.

I hold it gently in my hands and start to lick it. Long wet licks all the way from the base to the tip. Tracing a different path with my tongue each time. The dildo throbs in my hand and the sound of a piano thunking suddenly makes me giggle.

A few minutes later Harry opens my door. He stands there silhouetted in the doorframe. He doesn't turn the light on, but I know he can see me from the light from the hallway.

"Colby," he says warningly. His voice deep and his tone implying I'm in trouble.

I merely grin at him, hold his gaze and swallow the dildo down, taking it all the way to the back of my throat. I'm getting so much better at this. I pull it back out and hold it tauntingly close to my lips.

Harry groans, strides in, slams the door behind him and stalks up to the bed. He snatches the dildo from me and throws it aside. I wince, he is very trusting that it goes inert the moment no one is touching it. I'm not so sure I'd be so brave.

The sound of his fly unzipping catches my full, undivided attention. Then I lick my lips hungrily as he pulls out his full, heavy cock and offers me the real thing.

I crawl forward so that I can accept it. I mean, it would be rude not to, wouldn't it?

Thank You

Thank you for reading my book, I hope you enjoyed it!
Want more Colby & Harry?
How about a FREE exclusive bonus epilogue, where they make use of the rutting stool?

Tap the link to sign up to my monthly newsletter for instant access!

https://www.srodman.net/newsletter-sign-up.html

If you are already a subscriber, don't worry! The link was in the 21st March 2023 newsletter.
(If you signed up after that date, follow the link in your welcome email.)

Limited time offer **Not one, but TWO free books when you sign up!**
Sign up now and your welcome email will contain links not only for the bonus epilogue but also for a free copy of Incubus Broken and Omega Alone.

If none of that takes your fancy, how about exclusive short stories and opportunities to receive free copies of new books before they are released?

Sign up for my newsletter.

https://www.srodman.net/newsletter-sign-up.html

It comes out once a month, you can unsubscribe at any time and I never spam, because we all hate spam.

If the link is broken, please type www.srodman.net into your browser.

The Prince's Vessel

Coming soon

The penthouse is lovely. Floor to ceiling windows display a stunning view of London. The interior is all very modern and chic. I love coming to England.

The man fawning over me, gives yet another unnecessary bow. "Is everything to your satisfaction, your Highness?"

"Yes, thank you. Everything is quite lovely."

He bows again, and it is a struggle not to roll my eyes.

"Mr. Reynolds will be over at ten a.m tomorrow to go over the protocols for the King's coronation."

"Very well." I nod.

The man licks his lips. What is he hesitating for? A soft knock on the door answers my question. I sense beautiful magic. Its colors vibrant and vivid. Like the northern lights. I turn towards the door in excitement. A ripe vessel. Like no other I have ever sensed before.

My host scurries over and flings the door open. A young man steps inside. His aquamarine eyes meet mine steadily. His dark hair is tied up in an immaculate bun and I yearn to free it and discover how long it is. And then run my hands through it.

"Your Highness, may I introduce James Cambell, younger brother of Duke Sothbridge."

James inclines his head the bare minimum that could be considered polite.

"Pleased to meet you," I say with a grin.

He is gorgeous. His magic tastes divine, and he is of good stock. I think I might be smitten.

"Mr. Cambell can stay and provide you with company, unless you wish to be alone?"

"I'd be delighted if Mr. Cambell stayed."

James rolls his eyes. My host literally rubs his hands together in glee. I barely register him leaving until the door clicks shut.

James's eloquent fingers start undoing the dark jacket of his suit. "So, where do you want to fuck me?"

I feel my eyebrow raise as I meet his intense glare.

Gorgeous. Powerful and enticing magic. High born. And feisty. Scrub being smitten, I think I'm in love.

Books By S. Rodman

All my books can be found on my Amazon Author page HERE
Or view at www.srodman.net

Darkstar Pack

Evil Omega

Evilest Omega

Evil Overlord Omega

Duty & Magic: MM Modern Day Regency

Lord Garrington's Vessel

Earl Hathbury's Vessel

The Bodyguard's Vessel

Non Series

All Rail the King

Shipped: A Hollywood Gay Romance

Hunted By The Omega

Hell Broken

Past Life Lover

How to Romance an Incubus

Lost & Loved

Dark Mage Chained

Prison Mated

Incubus Broken

Omega Alone

Printed in Great Britain
by Amazon

36054757R00108